P9-ARG-960

KILLER
CUPID

Books by Laurien Berenson

Melanie Travis Mysteries

A PEDIGREE TO DIE FOR
UNDERDOG
DOG EAT DOG
HAIR OF THE DOG
WATCHDOG
HUSH PUPPY
UNLEASHED
ONCE BITTEN
HOT DOG
BEST IN SHOW
JINGLE BELL BARK
RAINING CATS AND DOGS
CHOW DOWN
HOUNDED TO DEATH
DOGGIE DAY CARE MURDER
GONE WITH THE WOOF
DEATH OF A DOG WHISPERER
THE BARK BEFORE CHRISTMAS
LIVE AND LET GROWL
MURDER AT THE PUPPY FEST
WAGGING THROUGH THE SNOW
RUFF JUSTICE
HERE COMES SANTA PAWS
BITE CLUB
GAME OF DOG BONES
HOWLOWEEN MURDER
PUP FICTION
SHOW ME THE BUNNY
KILLER CUPID

Peg and Rose Mysteries

PEG AND ROSE SOLVE A MURDER

Published by Kensington Publishing Corp.

KILLER
CUPID

LAURIEN
BERENSON

Kensington Publishing Corp.
www.kensingtonbooks.com

KENSINGTON BOOKS are published by

Kensington Publishing Corp.
119 West 40th Street
New York, NY 10018

All Kensington titles, imprints and distributed lines are available at special quantity discounts for bulk purchases for sales promotion, premiums, fund-raising, educational or institutional use. Special book excerpts or customized printings can also be created to fit specific needs. For details, write or phone the office of the Kensington Special Sales Manager: Kensington Publishing Corp., 119 West 40th Street, New York, NY, 10018. Attn. Special Sales Department. Phone: 1-800-221-2647.

The K and Teapot logo is a trademark of Kensington Publishing Corp.

Library of Congress Control Number: 2022943475

ISBN: 978-1-4967-4103-5

First Kensington Hardcover Edition: January 2023

ISBN: 978-1-4967-4105-9 (ebook)

10 9 8 7 6 5 4 3 2 1

Printed in the United States of America

For my wonderful husband Bruce.
You'll always be my Valentine.

KILLER
CUPID

Chapter
One

"I know something you don't know," Kevin announced.

Five years old, almost six, my son was a pint-sized bundle of energy and charm. He had his father's wicked sense of humor, deep blue eyes, and shaggy blond hair. Now, as I watched him dance gleefully around the front hall of our house, it occurred to me that his hair was overdue for a trim. Something else to add to our busy weekend schedule.

It was Saturday morning and I'd only been up and dressed for an hour. Already it felt as though the day might be getting away from me.

"What don't I know?" I asked Kevin.

"I can't tell you." He giggled. "It's a surprise!"

My life is full of surprises. Not all of them are good ones.

Judging by the expression on my son's face, however, this was a surprise I should be excited about. At least that was what he thought.

In our house, excitement is contagious. I heard the sound of scrambling feet. Kevin's frolicking had brought our canine crew running.

Five black Standard Poodles, all interrelated, all current or former show dogs, came bounding toward us from several directions. Bud, the small, spotted mutt we'd adopted several years earlier, brought up the rear on his much shorter legs.

I reached down, intending to swoop Kevin up before he could be bowled over by the oncoming horde. He dodged away, evading my grasp, and embraced the scrum eagerly. Tar and Augie were our two boisterous male Poodles. That pair led the charge. Eve and six-month-old puppy Plum raced close behind.

Following them was Faith, my very first Standard Poodle, and the dog who held my heart in her paws. Now in her senior years, Faith was often content to watch rather than take part in the youngsters' high jinks. As she entered the hall, Faith's dark eyes immediately found mine. When I held out a hand, she skirted around the edge of the room and came to my side.

Standards are the tallest variety of Poodles. The top of Faith's head nearly reached my waist. I could trail my fingers over the dense black curls on her back without leaning down. She pressed her body against my legs as Bud came skidding across the hardwood floor and leapt into the fray.

"What the heck is going on down there?"

My older son, Davey, leaned over the banister on the second floor to have a look. At fifteen, he was navigating the transition from child to adulthood. His voice seemed too deep for his lanky body, and his long limbs were always outgrowing his clothes. Now he frowned down at us and attempted to stand on his dignity.

"You people are crazy," he muttered.

My husband, Sam, stuck his head out of his home office. "You'd better hope not," he said. "Considering that we're your family. Because, you know . . . genetics." He strolled out to join us.

Kevin popped up out of the dog pile. "I told Mom we have a secret."

"Wait! What?" Davey came flying down the stairs. "You weren't supposed to do that."

"Do what?" Sam glanced my way. He and I have been married for eight years and I adore everything about him. Including his naive belief that I'm on top of everything that goes on in our house. "Do you know what this is about?"

"Not a clue," I told him.

Together, Sam and I turned and stared at Davey.

"What?" He held up his hands innocently. "I didn't say a thing."

"No, but you know something," I said.

"Davey knows lots of things," Kevin informed us. Now that the Poodle mayhem had finally died down, he was ready to tune back in to the conversation. "He's in high school."

Davey was generally a really good kid. But I'm a mother. So I had to ask. "Are you in trouble?"

"Whoa." Davey took a step back. "Where did that come from?"

Note that he hadn't answered my question.

"Kev says you have a secret."

"It's a surprise!" Kevin crowed. "A really fun one."

Sam and I both relaxed somewhat. Davey wasn't in the clear just yet, however. "Why don't you tell us about it?" Sam asked.

"He can't," Davey replied.

"Why not?"

"I promised," Kev said solemnly. "I crossed my heart."

I hunkered down to his level. "It isn't a good thing to keep secrets from your parents."

"It's not our fault," Davey told us.

"Then whose is it?" As soon as the words were out of my mouth, I suspected I already knew what his answer was going to be. Before he could reply, however, the doorbell rang.

Immediately the Poodles regrouped and raced to-

ward a new target. "Saved by the bell," Davey said
with a grin.

Sam was closer to the front of the hall than I was.
He glanced through the row of glass panes beside
the door before unlatching it and pulling it open.
The fact that he didn't say a word to the dogs who
were now milling around his legs confirmed my
guess. Aunt Peg—the Poodles' favorite person—had
arrived.

We hadn't been expecting visitors, but that never
seemed to matter where Aunt Peg was concerned. She
swept through life like a tornado, making grown men
tremble and thrusting all unwanted obstacles from
her path. The fact that she was in her seventies had
neither mellowed her disposition nor slowed her stride.
Aunt Peg did what she wanted, when she wanted, and
damn the consequences to anyone who attempted to
impede her progress.

The door drew open and a draft of cold air blew
into the hallway. It was early February and several
inches of new snow had fallen overnight. In a Connecticut winter, that was nothing out of the ordinary.

Aunt Peg stamped her booted feet on the front mat
before coming inside. She was appropriately bundled
up from head to toe. A longtime breeder of Standard
Poodles, Peg was now an acclaimed dog show judge.
So she'd had plenty of experience dealing with in-
clement weather.

Her eyes lit up when the Poodle pack came spilling out of the house. Of course she paused to greet the dogs first. Never mind that we—her human relatives—stood, shivering, only a few feet away.

"You're doing a good job with Plum's hair," Aunt Peg said to Sam. She aimed a wave in his direction. "It's coming along nicely."

Sam and I had whelped a litter of puppies for her the previous summer. Aunt Peg had kept a male she'd named Joker. Sam, who'd recently lost one of his older bitches, had chosen Plum for himself. Both puppies were now growing coat so they could begin their show careers in the spring.

"She'll be ready soon," Sam agreed. He drew Aunt Peg inside so he could close the door. The Poodles scrambled in quickly behind her.

"You lot." Aunt Peg motioned to the boys. "Come and give me a hug."

Kevin complied eagerly. Davey was only a step behind. At his age, he wasn't into hugging, but like the rest of us he knew better than to deny a request from Aunt Peg.

"You didn't say hello to Bud," Kevin complained when he'd extricated himself.

As she unzipped her parka, Aunt Peg looked down toward the floor at her feet. She stood six feet tall, so there was a fair bit of distance between her and the little mutt who was gazing up at her and wagging his stubby tail. Bud was a total chow hound. He was probably hoping Aunt Peg had a dog biscuit in her pocket.

"Bud's not a Poodle," she pointed out unnecessarily.

"He doesn't know that," Davey said with a laugh.

"Quite so." Aunt Peg reached down and ruffled the dog's ears.

Then she pulled off her parka and draped it over my arm. Her scarf followed. Her hat and gloves came next. I could have been a coatrack for all the notice she'd taken of me.

I shoved everything inside a nearby closet and said, "You have some explaining to do."

"Do I?" Aunt Peg's expression wasn't entirely innocent.

"Kevin says he has a secret," Sam told her. "We're assuming you had a hand in that."

"Perhaps." Aunt Peg favored us with an enigmatic smile. "Why don't we all sit down first?"

Sam and I herded everyone, dogs included, into the living room. Aunt Peg settled on the middle cushion of the couch. Eve and Augie hopped up to flank her sides. Plum lay down across Aunt Peg's feet.

As the rest of us found our seats, Faith looked at the other Poodles disdainfully and remained glued to my side. *Good girl.*

Aunt Peg waited until we were all settled and giving her our full attention. "I swore the boys to secrecy so we could all spring the surprise at the same time. As you know, next Sunday is Valentine's Day."

I sighed under my breath. Yet another thing I was behind in planning for.

I loved my husband dearly. I knew he felt the same way about me. We'd been together for nearly a dozen years, and married for much of that time. At this point, we didn't need the candy and flower industries to tell us that February 14 was the only important day for us to express how we felt about one another.

"Valentine's Day," Sam repeated. "Right."

I smothered a laugh. Apparently I wasn't the only one who'd forgotten.

"The boys had a wonderful idea about how the two of you might celebrate," Aunt Peg continued. "I agreed to help them execute it."

"Go on," I said cautiously.

Sam looked like a deer in headlights. I nearly laughed again.

"I came up with it." Davey sounded proud of himself.

"I helped too!" Kevin chimed in.

"The boys thought you would both enjoy getting away for a few days over the Valentine's Day weekend," Aunt Peg continued. "Isn't that splendid?"

Davey nodded vigorously in agreement. It occurred

to me that my child might be entirely too susceptible to advertising.

"And the three of us have found just the place. The White Birch Inn bills itself as a winter wonderland in the Berkshire Mountains of Massachusetts. Their website looks lovely." Aunt Peg threaded her fingers through Eve's topknot hair and smiled. "Despite its rustic name, the place is actually a full-scale resort offering cross-country skiing, tobogganing, and ice-skating among its many amenities. In honor of the upcoming holiday, the inn is hosting a romantic Valentine's getaway. At Davey's request—"

"And mine," Kev interjected.

Aunt Peg nodded. "—I've made a reservation for the two of you. You depart Thursday afternoon. It's a three-hour drive. You should be there in plenty of time for dinner. You'll return Sunday evening."

"But—" I sputtered, then voiced the first objection that came to mind. "I have to work on Friday."

"That's already been taken care of," Aunt Peg assured me. "I've spoken with Russell and you've been granted a personal day off."

Russell Hanover was the headmaster of Howard Academy, where I was employed as a special needs tutor. I loved my job. I adored working with children and being able to make a difference in their lives. There was no way I'd have ever asked Mr. Hanover for time off so I could go away on vacation.

Aunt Peg had surely realized that, which was why she'd taken matters into her own hands. She was not only a Howard Academy alumna, she was also a generous benefactor. And one of very few people I knew who were close enough to our distinguished headmaster to call him by his first name. Of course Mr. Hanover would have acceded to her wishes. He'd probably felt he had no choice.

"You work for yourself," Aunt Peg said to Sam. My husband was a freelance designer of computer software. "I'm assuming that a few days away from your desk won't break the bank?"

"Umm, no." Sam looked as stunned by this turn of events as I was.

"What about Davey and Kevin?" I asked.

"Aunt Peg is going to move in here while you're gone," Kevin said happily. "She'll take care of us."

"And your Poodles," Aunt Peg supplied.

"Including Bud," Davey added.

"What about your dogs?" I asked. Aunt Peg had three Standard Poodles of her own at home.

"They'll come with me, of course."

Oh my. This was a startling development. I could hardly begin to imagine how it was all going to work.

I gazed around the room at the three of them. "It will be chaos."

"We like chaos," Kevin said.

Of course they did. That was what I was afraid of. Well, one of the things anyway.

Faith had been lying on the floor beside my chair. Now, as if she understood what we were talking about, she sat up and placed her head in my lap. Her nose was slightly dry and her muzzle was gray with age. Once, our time together had seemed limitless. Now I cherished every moment. I rubbed Faith's cheek with my thumb, then scratched beneath her ears. She closed her eyes and sighed happily.

"I'm not going anywhere without Faith," I said.

"Certainly not," Aunt Peg replied. "I had a lovely chat with the inn's owner, Evelyn Barker, when I booked your reservation. She assured me that the White Birch Inn is a dog-friendly establishment and that Faith will be every bit as welcome there as you and Sam are."

Faith's pomponned tail swished back and forth on the rug. She liked the sound of that. As did I. I never should have doubted Aunt Peg. In her inimitable way, she'd already thought of everything.

Sam looked my way. "You and I have never been away on vacation without the boys. A long weekend at a romantic inn sounds like it could be fun. Just the two of us all on our own."

I nodded. He was right.

"About that," Aunt Peg said.

At this point, there was nothing I could do but laugh. "Now what?"

"You'll like this part," she told us.

One could only hope.

"Aunt Peg helped us get everything set up," Davey announced with a flourish. "And then we invited Uncle Frank and Aunt Bertie to join you."

Yet another pleasant surprise. This day was turning out to be full of them.

Chapter
Two

Five days later, I was sitting in the backseat of Sam's SUV on my way to the Berkshire Mountains. The weather was clear and cold, and traffic was scarce as we headed north from coastal Connecticut to western Massachusetts. It was a perfect day for making the long drive.

I'd have been sitting up front with Sam except that back here on the bench seat, Faith could lie down beside me with most of her body draped across my legs. My sister-in-law and good friend, Bertie, was riding shotgun. My brother, Frank, was sitting on Faith's other side. We'd only been on the road for half an hour and already Frank was squirming in his seat.

I glanced his way and frowned.

My brother hated sitting still. He'd always been impatient for *things to happen*. Despite our physical similarities—we shared the same tawny hair, slender build, and wide-set hazel eyes—our personalities couldn't have been more different. While I liked to work through problems, Frank preferred to circumvent them—even when the difficulties were ones he'd caused himself. When we were younger, I'd felt as though I was always rescuing him from one crisis or another.

Thankfully, those years were behind me now. Frank's marriage to Bertie and the subsequent births of their children, Maggie and Josh, had made him grow up in a hurry. Bertie loved my brother, but she was a practical woman—and too smart to let him get away with much. Once, it had seemed as though Frank and I were doomed to bring out the worst in each other, but now our relationship was better than it had ever been.

Even so, Frank returned my frown with a glare. "Your dog is taking up way too much space."

"Her name is Faith," I replied. Frank already knew that, but apparently he needed a reminder. "And she's hardly taking up any room at all. Most of her is in my lap."

"Not that huge tail." He gestured toward the fluffy black pompon that was hanging over the edge of the seat.

"Oh, please. It's nowhere near you."

"It would be if I stretched my legs."

"Then don't stretch them," I retorted.

"And to think," Bertie mused aloud up front, "I

was under the impression that we'd left all our squabbling children at home."

"I thought so too," Sam agreed. "You don't suppose they're going to be like this all weekend, do you?"

"I certainly hope not." Bertie lifted a sculpted brow.
With her auburn hair and curvaceous body, she was a
strikingly attractive woman. "Maybe we should put
on a cartoon back there to entertain them?"

Sam nodded. He and Bertie were both pointedly ig-
noring Frank and me. "That might work. If not, we
could try opening the back windows and letting them
hang their heads out."

Frank and I shared a look. I supposed we deserved
that.

"All right," I said. "You've made your point."

"We apologize," Frank grumbled.

Bertie swiveled in her seat to face us. "Good. Because I'm about to get out the itinerary of events I
downloaded from the inn's website. Who wants to
hear all about what they have lined up for us?"

"I do," I replied. "Aunt Peg mentioned there were
activities, but I never had a chance to see what they
were."

Bertie skimmed down the page she held in her
hand. "From the looks of this, there will be plenty of
ways for us to keep ourselves entertained. Among
other things, there's a wine tasting, a flower-arrang-

ing course, and even an opportunity to learn how to make fudge."

"That's for you," Sam told me. He was well aware of the sweet tooth I'd developed from hanging around Aunt Peg.

"I don't know if I want to know how to *make* fudge," I said. "But eating it is a definite yes."

Bertie was still reading. "There will be candlelight dinners, hot toddies in front of the fire, hiking, skating, and the chance to sign up for a moonlight sleigh ride. The inn's amenities include an indoor swimming pool, an outdoor hot tub, a full-service spa, and an indoor/outdoor terraced bar that overlooks the mountain."

"The place must be huge," said Sam. "It sounds as though they have something there for everyone."

"What it sounds like is perfection." Frank sighed happily. "Once we get there, I may never want to leave."

"Oh honey." Bertie reached around and patted his knee. "It's sweet that you think you'll have a choice."

Dusk had fallen by the time we arrived at the White Birch Inn. My first glimpse of the resort from the foot of its long driveway nearly took my breath away. Nestled at the bottom of a snow-covered mountain, it was a white-shingled, colonial style building standing at least three stories tall. A wide portico, flanked by columns, covered the double front door. The porch above it provided a view of the circular driveway at the entrance. Numerous chimneys dotted the inn's extensive roofline.

From afar, the building glowed in the semidarkness. Warm light filled its many windows. Strings of fairy lights decorated its shutters and eaves. As the moon began its ascent in the sky, the White Birch Inn glittered against its snowy backdrop like a fairy-tale castle come to life.

"Wow." Frank leaned up from the backseat for a better view.

"I'll echo that sentiment," said Sam. Even Faith sat up to take a look.

There was snow all around us, but the driveway was freshly plowed. Moments later, we pulled up before the front door. Before the SUV had even stopped moving, a bellman was already hurrying out to get our bags. A parking attendant was right behind him. As Sam handed over his keys, I fastened a leash to Faith's collar and hopped her out of the car.

Faith gave herself a long, leisurely shake. It began at her nose and finished at the tip of her tail. That done, she gazed at her new surroundings eagerly. Faith was always up for a new adventure.

"This will be your home for the next few days," I told her. "They like dogs here, so you might even make some new friends."

I took Faith around the corner so she could have a quick potty break. Then we returned to the front of the building and caught up with Sam. He was waiting for us just outside the front door. Bertie and Frank had already gone ahead inside. Nevertheless Sam paused before following them.

"I've been wondering about something," he said. "You and I have been sent here for a three-day vacation devoted to romance. Do you suppose Peg was trying to imply anything by that?"

"I should hope not." I looped an arm around his waist. "What Aunt Peg doesn't know about our love life is pretty much everything. Which suits me just fine."

Sam nodded in agreement.

"Don't forget, the idea for this trip originated with the boys. Aunt Peg just helped them make the arrangements."

"Hmm." He considered for a moment. "Maybe the kids were trying to get rid of us so they could cut loose for a few days."

The thought made me laugh. "If that's the case, they'll end up regretting their plan. I've stayed with Aunt Peg on occasion. It's like living with a drill sergeant."

The door in front of us opened. Bertie stuck her head out. "Hurry up, you two. Frank wants to get checked in so we can go exploring."

The inn's lobby was warm and spacious. There was a soaring two-story ceiling and a massive stone fireplace in the wall across from the front desk. A curved double staircase with spiral banisters led to the second floor. Above the center of the room was a chandelier constructed of antlers and lit by dozens of electric candles. The space was decorated in jewel tones; sapphire and emerald-green predominated. There were several cozy groupings of armchairs, and two overstuffed love seats had been positioned to take full advantage of the blazing fire.

Sam headed toward the front desk. I started to follow, but instead Faith pulled me in the direction of the hearth. I quickly saw why. There was a large dog bed on the floor near a stack of firewood. A thick-coated white dog was asleep there, his fluffy tail curled forward to cover his nose. Sensing Faith's presence as we drew near, the dog raised his head and pricked his ears.

To my surprise, he appeared to be smiling at us. Then I abruptly realized why. The dog was a Samoyed. That was one of the characteristics of that graceful, Nordic breed.

A woman walked over to stand beside me. She was tall and slim, dressed in a taupe cashmere dress that fell to the tops of her knee-high leather boots. Her make-up was deftly understated and her dark hair was gathered into an elegant chignon. I guessed she was in her fifties, but her look was timeless.

"You're about to meet Sammy," she said. "He feels it's his duty to personally greet every canine visitor to the inn."

"Sammy." I smiled at the white dog as he rose to his feet and stretched. "For a Samoyed?"

"He was my son's dog and he named him, so I didn't have a choice." The woman shrugged as if to say, *what can you do?* "Is your Poodle friendly?"

"Very friendly. Her name is Faith, and she likes everyone."

The two dogs approached each other with their tails high in the air. They sniffed noses briefly, exchanging a silent message only they understood. A moment later, both tails began to wag. *Mission accomplished.*

"That went well." The woman held out her hand. "I'm Evelyn Barker, owner and manager. It's a pleasure to meet you and welcome you to the White Birch Inn."

"Melanie Travis," I replied as we shook hands. "That's my husband, Sam Driver, checking in at the desk. I believe you spoke with my Aunt Peg on the phone last week."

Evelyn's lips quirked. "I did indeed. She's a formidable woman."

"That's one word for it."

"She grilled me quite thoroughly before deciding

that the accommodations would be suitable for your Standard Poodle."

"She would," I said. "Dogs are important to her."

"Yes, I got that impression. And Faith is definitely a welcome guest. I pride myself on hosting a pet-friendly resort, but not all dogs arrive as well trained as your big Poodle."

"People! New arrivals! Step this way please."

The voice behind me was high-pitched and sounded nervous. I turned around and saw a young woman with curly hair and bright red lipstick standing at the other end of the lobby. She was holding up a clipboard in front of her like a shield. As she tapped a pen impatiently against the metal clip, I saw that her crimson nail polish matched the shade on her lips.

Not satisfied with the alacrity of our response, the woman slipped the clipboard under her arm and clapped her hands together briskly. Beside me, Evelyn sighed under her breath. I looked at her questioningly.

"That's Belinda Rush, our events coordinator. She's wonderful at organizing things and making sure everyone knows where they're supposed to be. But sometimes I think her people skills could use some help."

You think?

Frank and Bertie were already heading Belinda's way. Sam, having finished checking in, came to collect me and Faith. I introduced him to Evelyn.

"It looks like we're being summoned," he said.

Evelyn nodded. "Belinda wants to make sure you're aware of all the activities you can sign up for this weekend. Our goal is to provide each couple with a wonderful Valentine's holiday experience, and we'd hate for you to regret missing out on something. The festivities begin tonight at seven in our dining room. Our first evening's event is a 'Date Night.'"

"Date night?" Sam repeated. "You mean like dinner and movie?"

"Precisely." Evelyn smiled. "We've found that offering something simple on the first night makes it easier for everyone to settle in and relax after the trip they've made to get here. After dinner, we'll be screening *Casablanca* in our activities room. I hope you'll join us."

"Definitely," I said. "I love that movie."

"That settles it." Sam sounded just as pleased by the prospect as I was. "It's a date."

Chapter
Three

Up close Belinda looked even more jittery than she had from across the room. There were dark circles under her eyes and a nervous smile came and went as she introduced herself. I wondered how old she was. Certainly not more than twenty-five. Maybe this was her first real job and she was worried about making a good impression.

It took the four of us ten minutes to get signed up for a selection of the inn's upcoming activities. By that time, a line of incoming guests had begun to form behind us. Belinda noted that. She was ready to move us along.

"I'll print up schedules and have them delivered to your rooms," she said. "Do you have any questions?"

"Just one," said Bertie. "What happens if we change our minds later?"

"Umm . . ." Belinda blinked several times. Her teeth

began to gnaw on her lower lip. "Why would you want to do that?"

"Suppose the weather is frigid when I signed up to go tobogganing. Maybe I'll decide I'd rather settle down in the library with a good book instead."

"Oh. Okay." Belinda looked down at her clipboard as if she thought she might find the answer there. "That shouldn't be a problem. I mean, you're here to have a great time, right? So whatever works out best for you is fine by us. And sometimes . . ."

She leaned closer to our small group and said in a confidential tone, "Sometimes on weekends like this one, guests don't show up for their scheduled activities at all because, you know . . ."

Bertie looked at her blankly.

"Umm . . ." Color rose in Belinda's cheeks as she struggled to find the right words. "It's almost Valentine's Day—and we're all in favor of romance here at the White Birch Inn. It might happen, even in the middle of the day, that couples get to feeling a little frisky . . . if you see what I mean?"

Bertie snorted out a laugh that was quickly contained. She assumed a more serious expression. "I do. But you don't have to worry about us. Frank and I have young children at home. Afternoon sex is so far in our past, it isn't even a blip on our radar anymore."

Frank made a strangled sound. He averted his eyes and stared at the ceiling. Who knew he was such a prude? Beside me, Sam appeared to be enjoying Frank's discomfort just as much as I was.

Bertie reached over to give her husband's hand a squeeze. It didn't help. Instead Frank used that hold to pull her out of line. The two of them strode quickly to the wide staircase that led to the inn's upper floors.

"Frisky," Sam said under his breath, when we'd caught up to them. He did a little dance on the steps. "I like the sound of that." His voice lowered to a pseudo-sexy tone. "Hey babe, when we get to our room, do you wanna get *frisky*?"

Frank forestalled my reply by heaving a loud sigh. "I'm never going to hear the end of this, am I?"

"Probably not," I told him. "Not this weekend, anyway."

Our rooms were side by side at the end of the west wing on the second floor. As Sam opened the door, I unhooked Faith's leash. She darted past us and jumped up onto the down comforter that covered the king-sized bed. Despite Faith's age, sometimes she acted just like a little kid.

While Faith made herself comfortable, I took a look around. The room's decor echoed the warm hues from the lobby, with the addition of a few tartan accents. Aside from the bed, there was a sculpted pine dresser with a flat screen TV on the wall above it and a cozy love seat complete with a reading lamp. The tub in the bathroom looked easily big enough for two people to share.

The sight of those comforts paled, however, beside the view that was visible through the double windows on the rear wall of the room. For a full minute, I just stood and stared. All the resort's outdoor lights were on. The slope of the mountain, magnificent in all its snow-covered glory, looked as though it was mere inches away.

"Wow," I exhaled slowly.

Sam nodded. "I know. It makes you feel small, doesn't it?"

"It makes my problems feel small. That's even better."

"Problems?" He turned my way. "You're supposed to be off duty this weekend. That means you shouldn't have brought any problems with you."

I'm a mother. And a teacher. So there are always issues niggling in the back of my mind. But Sam was right. Maybe none of them were pressing enough that they couldn't be put aside for now.

"Off duty sounds like a great idea to me," I said. Immediately I felt lighter. Until this moment, I'd had no idea how much I needed this vacation.

Sam walked over to the low table in front of the love seat. "Look what our hosts left for us."

I'd been so distracted by the view that I'd obviously missed out on several important details inside the room. Now I noticed the crystal vase holding half a dozen red roses on the night table beside the bed. They had to be the reason the space smelled so heavenly. And Sam was standing beside an ice bucket with the foil-wrapped top of a champagne bottle peeking out over its rim. Nearby, two crystal flutes were tied together by a silky red bow. Next to them was a small silver tray holding two bowls and a dog biscuit for Faith.

I was already heading that way. "Are those strawberries?"

Sam grinned wickedly. "And whipped cream."

Almost there, I was momentarily sidetracked by a wicker basket on top of the dresser. "Bubble bath," I said, sifting through the contents. "Massage oils, a shea butter scrub, lavender soap, his-and-hers loofahs. I think I've died and gone to heaven."

Sam crossed the room and locked the door. Then he turned to me and waggled his eyebrows suggestively. "Not quite yet, but I have an idea how we can work on that."

I bubbled out a laugh. "Is that an invitation to get frisky?"

Hands outstretched, fingers beckoning, Sam walked slowly toward me. "Try me," he said.

So we were late for dinner.

More than two dozen tables were scattered around the spacious dining room on the first floor of the inn. The tablecloths and napkins were snowy white. Tall candles and a bowl of fresh flowers adorned each tabletop. Our feet sank into the plush carpet as Sam and I hurried across the room. Bertie and Frank were waiting for us at our table.

Bertie was smirking when we slipped into our seats ten minutes after our reservation time. Frank just looked resigned.

"Don't say it," he grumbled.

"I wouldn't dream of it," I replied.

Bertie reached over and touched my cheek with the tip of her finger. "Something went right. Your face is glowing."

I picked up my menu and perused the options. "Shea butter scrub."

"Is that *all*?" she inquired.

Sam lowered his menu. "And whipped cream."

"You people are going to be the death of me," said Frank.

The three of us laughed. Frank glared around the table. He actually looked like he meant it. That made us laugh even harder.

Eventually things settled down and we all opted to try the chef's recommended menu. It was an excellent choice. We dined on white truffle risotto, followed by seared scallops and fresh asparagus. Then we ended our meal with coffee and a decadent mocha mousse. My plan to taste everything in moderation quickly went out the window. If the level of cuisine remained this high all week, I was going to have to let out all my clothes when I got home.

The activities room, where the movie would be shown, was on the lower level of the inn. When Sam, Bertie, Frank, and I left the dining room to go downstairs, most of the other couples were heading in the same direction. I wasn't surprised that *Casablanca* was a popular choice. Pairing Ingrid Bergman and Humphrey Bogart in the story of star-crossed lovers had never failed to leave me sniffling by the end.

The activities room turned out to be a large, brightly lit space, currently filled with rows of chairs. A bar had been set up at the back of the room. The bartender there was already busy filling orders. A nearby popcorn machine was also doing a brisk business. The buttered popcorn smelled delicious, but after the wonderful meal we'd just eaten, I was too full to want anything else.

While Frank and Bertie went to get drinks, Sam and I chose seats for the four of us in the middle of the room. People were still strolling in, and the lights had yet to be lowered. We had at least a few more minutes before the movie would begin.

"Do you think I should run up and check on Faith?" I asked Sam before we sat down. I'd already fed Faith before we had our own dinner. When Sam and I left the room the big Poodle had been snoozing on our bed.

"I wouldn't. She's probably still asleep up there. If you go wake her up, she'll be unhappy when you leave again."

Of course, he was right. I slipped into the row of seats and sat down. "In that case, I'll just take her outside for a last walk after the movie ends."

Two couples came down the aisle together and took seats in front of us. The men sat next to each other, as did the two women. The men immediately began to discuss sports. The women appeared to be comparing their manicures. I bit back a laugh and wondered how their romantic weekend was shaping up.

The lights in the room began to dim. Sam got up and went to see what was keeping Frank and Bertie. Being a naturally snoopy person, I tuned in to the conversation in front of me.

"I am *not* happy," one woman said under her breath to the other. "I booked this getaway before Christmas. You know how Ralph is. It's like pulling teeth to get him to take time off."

Her friend nodded sympathetically.

"I was promised a room with a mountain view. *Promised*. And instead, what do our windows face? The swimming pavilion. As if anyone would want to look at that."

"We have the same view from our room," the friend ventured. "I don't mind it."

The first woman snorted derisively. Clearly her friend's opinion wasn't important. "Ralph and I drove all the way up here from the city. When I look out my window, I want to see a mountain."

The mountain view *was* pretty spectacular. Then again, here in the Berkshires there were mountains all around us. Maybe the woman should try looking out another window? Somehow I doubted that would be a welcome suggestion.

"It's all Belinda's fault," the woman snapped. "She's the one handling the arrangements. I don't care how busy she thinks she is. She shouldn't make promises if she can't deliver."

"Maybe you should file a complaint," her friend said mildly.

"I might do that. You just see if I don't."

Initially the two women had been whispering. Gradually, however, their voices had risen. Since this was one of Belinda's planned events, it would make sense for her to be here. I hoped she wasn't near enough to hear what was being said about her.

I swiveled in my chair and looked around the

room. Frank, Bertie, and Sam were finally on their way back to our seats. Frank was holding two cocktails. Bertie had her hands full with a double-sized bag of popcorn. Sam was carrying a pair of liqueurs. He preferred Grand Marnier. I hoped he'd chosen Amaretto for me.

My gaze skimmed across the rear of the room, then abruptly stopped. Belinda was there, thankfully too far away to have overheard the women's conversation. The movie was about to begin. She was surveying the audience as everyone hurried to find their seats.

I was about to turn away when someone else caught my eye. As the light turned to shadow, an attractive man dressed in a ski sweater and corduroy slacks strolled over to where Belinda was standing. Long dark hair curled around his collar; his coffee-brown eyes looked nowhere but at her.

Casually, the man stopped beside Belinda. She didn't acknowledge his presence. Instead she continued to stare straight ahead, looking out over the room. The pair were so close to each other that their shoulders and arms were touching. And Belinda made no attempt to move away. I saw his fingers reach toward hers—

"I know you said you didn't want anything," Sam said as he slipped into his seat. "But when in Rome . . ."

"Amaretto?" Even as I reached for the glass, I could already smell the liqueur's distinctive almond scent.

"Of course."

"I love you," I said.

"That's the plan." Sam lifted his glass and we clinked together lightly. "Here's looking at you, Kid."

I had to laugh. "That's a terrible Humphrey Bogart impression."

Sam just shrugged. "Maybe so, but unlike the guy Bogart plays in the movie, I get the girl in the end."

"I'll drink to that," I said.

Chapter
Four

"*Casablanca* is my favorite movie," I said happily.

Sam and I were holding hands as we climbed the staircase back to the second floor. It was nearly eleven o'clock. I hoped Faith was still napping. Otherwise, she'd be wondering where we were. If Sam and I were home, we'd already have been in bed for the night by now.

I released Sam's hand and slipped my arm around his waist. Then I lowered my voice and said, "Louis, I think this is the beginning of a beautiful friendship."

He laughed. "And you thought my Bogart impression was bad."

"It's not the voice that matters," I said in a lofty tone. "It's the words."

"Oh." Sam still sounded amused. "In that case, I thought we already had a beautiful friendship."

"We'll always have Paris," I said dreamily.

He looked down at me. "Just how many glasses of Amaretto did you have tonight?"

"Two." I straightened to walk down the hallway beside him. "It was a long movie. And besides, I'm on vacation."

"Try telling that to Faith."

As Sam slipped the keycard into its slot, we both heard the sound of the Poodle whining just inside the door. When it unlocked, I pushed it open and dropped to my knees. Faith leapt directly into my arms.

"I'm sorry," I crooned into her ear as she and I hugged each other. "I know that was a long time to leave you alone in a strange place."

Of course Faith forgave me. Dogs don't carry a grudge. All that mattered was that we were back now. And that I was about to take her outside for a delayed run.

Sam scooped Faith's leash up off the dresser and tossed it to me. "Want me to come with you?"

"No, we'll be fine on our own. This won't take long." I slipped my feet into a pair of boots and grabbed a wool scarf and down parka out of the closet by the door. "Even outside, this place is lit up like a Christmas tree. I'll just give Faith a quick run around behind the inn."

"Take your phone with you."

I patted my pocket. "Got it."

"And don't get into any trouble."

"Who me?" The question didn't sound nearly as innocent as I'd hoped it might.

Sam started to frown. I took that as a good time for Faith and me to make our escape. By the time I closed the door behind me, the Poodle was already halfway down the empty hallway. Her leash dangled uselessly from my hand as I hurried to catch up.

"Hey you," I called as Faith romped her way to the staircase. "Wait for me. We're supposed to be attached."

Her tail was high in the air. It swished smartly from side to side. I couldn't blame Faith for wanting to lead the way. This late at night, she had every right to be impatient.

At the top of the steps, I snapped the leash to her collar. The connection barely slowed Faith down. We'd almost reached the lobby when Sammy came bounding out from behind the front desk. The white dog issued a short, sharp bark of greeting.

"Sammy, shush!" Evelyn was sitting near the fireplace. There was an open book in her lap. She rose and turned to see what had caught her dog's attention.

"Oh good, it's you," she said with a smile. "I was afraid he was barking at one of the less amenable guests. Can you believe there was a man who checked in this afternoon and asked me if Sammy was part polar bear? I thought at first that he was joking, but apparently not."

Evelyn and I laughed together.

"Are Faith and Sammy the only two dogs here at the moment?" I asked.

She nodded. "During the summer when families come to stay, they're more inclined to bring pets with them. But couples planning to celebrate Valentine's Day rarely think to include their dogs."

While we were talking, Faith and Sammy had renewed their budding friendship. Sammy danced around Faith, then crouched down on the floor and issued an invitation to play.

"I was about to take Faith outside for a walk," I told her. "Would Sammy like to come with us? I'm sure Faith would enjoy running around with him."

"He'd love that." Evelyn walked over. "Playing in the snow is Sammy's favorite thing. Unfortunately, I'm often too busy to indulge him—especially this week with everything we have going on. You're sure you don't mind?"

"Not at all. As long as he'll come back to me when I call him?"

"Maybe not the first time," Evelyn admitted. "Sammy does love cold weather. But once he realizes you're serious, he'll buckle down and pay attention. Especially if he's already enjoyed a good run."

A door at the rear of the lobby led to a wide porch

that ran along the back of the inn. It overlooked a spacious snow covered meadow. The ice-skating pond was off to one side in the distance. The view must have been gorgeous in summer. Even now in February, weatherproof furniture was set out for guests who didn't mind weathering the brisk temperatures.

The inn was built on a slight slope, so from the porch we had to descend another set of steps to reach the open area behind it. Sammy flew down the stairs and immediately raced away. Faith watched him go, whining impatiently under her breath. As soon as I unsnapped her leash, she took off too.

Though there were plenty of lights on behind the inn, the outdoor space was large enough to still contain pockets of darkness. It was easy for me to keep track of Faith. Her black coat stood out against the snowy backdrop. Sammy was a different story. He blended in. As the two dogs raced around the perimeter of the field, there were several times when I thought I'd lost him. Then he'd leap in the air and I'd be able to pick him out again.

The dogs were having so much fun together that I hated to call them back. But in the dark, I didn't want to let them get too far away from me either. The only cleared pathway on this side of the inn was the one that led to the skating pond. Hoping to close the distance between myself and the romping dogs, I headed that way.

The path was wide and well maintained. It looked as though it had been sanded earlier in the day. But now, as the temperature dropped, it was icing over again. Even wearing sturdy boots, I needed to step carefully and watch where I was going.

I hadn't gone far when I paused to check on the dogs' whereabouts. They were fine, but a movement in the other direction drew my attention. There was a small, unlit outbuilding on this side of the pond, presumably a skating shack where ice skates could be put on and taken off. But no one was skating on the pond now. A sign at the end of the path announced that it was currently closed.

That was enough to make me take a second look. Two people were just barely visible near the wall of the building. Their arms were wrapped around each other in what appeared to be an intimate embrace. It was clear that they wouldn't have wanted to be interrupted.

The pair were so engrossed in each other that they were oblivious to my presence. I had every intention of keeping it that way. Hugging the shadows, I quickly began to backpedal. Seconds later, Sammy began to bark. The couple abruptly broke apart. The man looked out across the snowy expanse and saw the dogs gamboling in the drifts.

Moving as one, the pair slipped around the corner of the wooden shack. Just before they disappeared from view, a shaft of light from an overhead flood lamp fell across their faces. The furtive couple were Belinda Rush and the man I'd seen her with earlier.

I wondered why they were outside at this time of night. What I'd witnessed looked like an assignation. But surely they could have found a warmer place to meet. And one with more privacy. Maybe the man also worked at the inn and relationships between employees were forbidden? Or maybe one or both of them were married?

As I retraced my steps on the icy path, I gave myself a mental kick. I didn't need answers. What I'd seen was none of my business.

I was almost back to the inn when Faith and Sammy came running to join me. Faith's black coat was covered with snow. Sammy's pink tongue was hanging out the side of his mouth. Both dogs looked inordinately pleased with themselves. Together we tromped across the hard-packed snow toward the stairs.

The dogs ran on ahead, but something made me pause and glance up. A row of multipaned windows above me was lit from within. Someone was standing outlined in one of the rectangles of yellow light. After a moment, I realized it was Evelyn.

I thought at first she might be checking on Sammy, but she wasn't. She wasn't looking at me either. Instead Evelyn was staring off into the distance, her gaze directed toward the small, darkened building beside the skating pond.

I woke up the next morning when Sam jumped out of bed and went to the window. Sleepily I raised my head and looked at him. This was the first morning in forever that I didn't have to get up early for work, or to get the boys ready for school, or because Bud was telling me that his tiny bladder needed to go outside *right now*.

"What's the matter?" I asked.

"I hear sirens. Don't you?"

"I'm trying not to." I flopped back down on the pillow. I closed my eyes. It didn't help. Those were sirens, all right. And it sounded as though they were coming closer. That didn't bode well.

"There are two sheriff cars," Sam said. "They turned off their sirens when they left the road. Now they're coming up the driveway."

"I hope nothing's wrong."

He turned and looked at me.

"Okay, I hope nothing's wrong that affects us. Is that better?"

Someone knocked on our door. Sam grabbed a robe and pulled it on. When he went to answer the door, Faith padded along behind him. She woofed happily as our visitor came striding into the room.

Bertie was dressed in some kind of stretchy outfit,

and she had running shoes on her feet. Her long hair was gathered up in a knit cap on her head. I was guessing she'd just finished her daily three-mile run. And she wasn't even breathing hard. All at once I felt like a slug.

Bertie patted Faith on the head before looking over at me. "Something's going on. The police are here."

"We just heard." I sat up in bed, covers pooling around my waist. It looked as though I was finished sleeping. "What did you see outside?"

"Nothing. I'd just gotten back to my room when they arrived. Frank's in the shower, so I figured I'd come over here and see if you guys knew anything." She looked at me pointedly.

"*Really?*" I grumbled

"What? You always know things. In fact, if there's trouble around you're usually right in the middle of it."

"I was asleep," I said.

"As if that's an excuse," Bertie sniffed.

"Maybe we should go downstairs and see what's happening," said Sam.

"Maybe we should get dressed first," I pointed out.

"That too." Sam turned to Bertie. "Let's all meet in the lobby in fifteen minutes. With luck, this will be a false alarm and we can go grab some breakfast."

"Make it eighteen," I said. "I'll need to run Faith outside first."

In the end, twenty minutes had passed before we

all met up again. I'd tried to take Faith out the same rear door we'd used the night before, but this time a young sheriff's deputy was blocking our path.

"I'm sorry, ma'am," he said. "But this area is currently off limits."

I attempted to peer around him. "Is something wrong?"

"Are you an employee of the inn?"

"No, I'm a guest. My husband and I are here for the long weekend."

"In that case, someone will update you shortly. In the meantime, you'll need to find another place to walk your dog."

"Yes, sir," I said.

By the time Faith and I returned, not only were Sam, Bertie, and Frank waiting in the lobby, but a number of the inn's other guests were there too. At least twenty people were milling around—all of them wondering, like we were, why the police had been called to the inn.

"I'm sure it's nothing," said an older man with a neatly clipped white beard. "Probably just a routine check."

His wife was clinging to his arm as if she was afraid he might get away from her. "Don't be ridiculous, Roger. Even in a little backwater town like this, nobody would turn on their sirens for a routine check."

Sam and I exchanged a look. We agreed with her.

There was a paneled door next to the front desk marked OFFICE. It opened, and Evelyn and a woman in a sheriff's uniform walked out together. Evelyn's face was pale. Her hands were clasped so tightly together that her knuckles were white. She seemed surprised to see so many people in the lobby.

Abruptly Evelyn stopped walking. Everyone turned to face her.

She cleared her throat, then said, "I apologize for the disturbance. I'm afraid I have some distressing news. There has been a death at the inn overnight. This is Sheriff Anne Finley. She and her team will be investigating to determine what happened. This shouldn't affect your vacations in any way. All of our Valentine's Day events will proceed as planned."

Suddenly, everyone was speaking at once. After a few moments, one voice rose above the rest. "Investigating?" a man called out. "Does that mean you're talking about a suspicious death?"

Someone gasped. A different man swore under his breath. Several women inched closer to their husbands.

Sheriff Finley stepped forward. She was a middle-aged, solidly built woman with a commanding presence. Her blue uniform fit as though it had been tailored to her. Immediately the room quieted.

"I'm afraid we don't have much information for you yet," she said in a clear voice. "But there's no need for anyone to be alarmed. Under Massachusetts law, any unattended death must be investigated, even if the person appears to have died of natural causes."

"Is that the case in this instance?" someone asked.

Evelyn spoke up before the sheriff had a chance to answer. "Yes," she replied firmly. "This was nothing more than an unfortunate accident brought about by the frigid weather. One of our staff members passed away from exposure to the elements."

Sheriff Finley shot Evelyn a look. Her lips pursed. For a moment, it looked as though she might say something. Then she thought better of it and remained silent.

"Who was it?" asked another guest.

"I'm afraid it's someone many of you will have met," Evelyn said unhappily. "The deceased is our events coordinator, Belinda Rush."

Chapter
Five

"What a shocking thing to have happen," Bertie said.

After the crowd downstairs had dispersed, the four of us and Faith had returned to Sam's and my room. Some of the other guests had gone to the dining room where breakfast was being served. But after what we'd heard, none of us were hungry anymore.

Now I frowned, thinking back to the scene I'd stumbled upon the night before. Belinda and someone else—a man—both of them out in the cold. Presumably he'd managed to safely make it back inside the inn.

Frank was sitting beside Bertie on the love seat. "What are the chances?" he muttered. Then his gaze swung my way. "Oh. Right."

"Cut that out." I was perched on the bed with my arm around Faith. "It's not like I'm some kind of harbinger of doom. We were just unlucky to be here when something unfortunate happened."

"It could be luck had nothing to do with it," said Bertie.

"What do you mean?" Sam asked. He was staring out the window. Unless Belinda's death had taken place at the foot of the mountain, I didn't think he could see much.

"Yesterday afternoon, when you and Sam were"— Bertie paused meaningfully—"doing whatever you were doing, Frank and I went on a tour of the premises. I'd read on the website that there would be a selection of pop-up shops here in case anyone wanted to buy last minute Valentine's Day gifts."

"And you know Bertie," Frank said. "She likes to shop."

His wife reached over and smacked his arm. Frank jumped in his seat. Then he deliberately removed himself to the other end of the love seat.

As if that would help.

"There's a ballroom downstairs near the lobby. Lots of vendors have booths set up in there," she continued. "Jewelry makers, flower sellers, chocolatiers, all sorts of things."

"Everyone was handing out free samples," Frank said.

Of course that was the part my brother would like.

"You should have seen him." Bertie frowned. "I nearly had to drag him away from the bourbon distillery booth."

"They kept offering me more stuff to taste," Frank said in his own defense. "Did you know bourbon comes in different flavors?"

"We did, actually." Sam turned away from the window. "What does that have to do with Belinda Rush's death?"

"Some of the vendors were complaining about the competition," Bertie told us. "The distiller said he'd only agreed to come because he was told he'd have the only booth offering an alcoholic beverage."

"But there was also a vintner in the room selling premium wines," Frank chimed in. Presumably he'd tasted samples there too.

"Even worse," he added, "someone had the dumb idea to place the man selling chocolates right next to a woman who was making fudge. Those two didn't look too pleased with each other either."

"Since Belinda was the event coordinator, it's likely she was the one who booked the concessions," I mused. "Maybe she thought she'd be able to attract a better selection of vendors if each one was convinced their product would be the only one of its kind."

"If that's the case, she lied to them," Bertie said. "Think about it. How mad would you be if you

schlepped all your stuff out here to the middle of nowhere only to find out that you'd been duped?"

"I'd probably be livid," I replied.

"Death by chocolate." Sam grimaced. "How very
appropriate for Valentine's Day."

"Death by whiskey sounds better," Frank said. Nobody was amused.

Sam came over and sat down on Faith's other side.
"If the vendors are angry and it's Belinda's fault, I'd
imagine the sheriff will look into that."

"Not if she decides that Belinda's death was an accident," Bertie said. "Downstairs, Evelyn seemed
pretty sure that was the case."

"Although Sheriff Finley didn't seem as convinced,"
I said. "Did you see the look on her face when Evelyn
was talking?"

"Then why didn't she speak up?" asked Frank.

"This is a small town," Sam pointed out. "And
possibly one that's heavily dependent upon the inn as
both its main tourist attraction and source of employ-
ment. I'm betting it's in both their best interests to
downplay what happened until they have more information."

"About that . . ." I said.

Three heads turned my way. Bertie looked curious,
Frank resigned. Sam's eyes were narrowed. That wasn't
a good sign.

"I might have some."

"Some what?" asked Bertie.

I swallowed and said, "More information."

Now Sam was staring at me. "How?"

"That's not possible," Frank protested. "We barely even knew the woman. And until twenty minutes ago, we had no idea she was dead."

"Even so," I admitted.

The three of them looked incredulous. In their position, I'd probably feel the same way.

"Maybe it's nothing," I said.

"Nope." Bertie was firm about that. "It's not nothing. Knowing you, it's definitely *something*."

Sam nodded. "After Evelyn finished speaking, the sheriff invited anyone who had information to come and see her. So I guess you'd better go down there."

I was already getting up from the bed. "Will you keep an eye on Faith for me?"

"Of course." Sam was almost as fond of Faith as I was. "Just don't let yourself get mixed up in anything you don't want to be part of."

"Of course not," I replied.

Sam didn't look convinced. This not being our first rodeo, I could understand why. I wasn't entirely convinced myself.

The lobby was empty when I arrived. Nevertheless, Evelyn was hovering behind the front desk as if she expected to be called upon imminently to do some-thing. I could hear the clink of cutlery within the din-ing room, and a low hum of conversation coming from the direction of the ballroom. It appeared that most guests had followed Evelyn's directive and opted not to let the unfortunate incident infringe upon their enjoyment of the holiday weekend.

Not Evelyn, though. She still looked stressed.

Sammy was lying in his bed beside the fireplace. I stopped to give him a pat before approaching the desk. Evelyn's eyes followed my progress around the room, but she didn't say a word until I was standing right in front of her.

"Can I help you?" she asked.

"Yes. I'd like to have a word with Sheriff Finley."

A look of surprise chased across Evelyn's face. She hadn't expected that. Then she quickly wiped her ex-pression clean.

"Of course." She smiled faintly. Evelyn was in the hospitality business. This was a request she could grant. "The sheriff is using my office to interview members of the staff. I'll slot you in next. It should only be a few minutes until she's ready for you."

"Thanks."

Evelyn looked at me curiously. Today she was wearing an azure silk scarf over a wool cable knit tunic. The ends of the scarf looked frayed, as if she might have been picking at them. "Is there anything I can do to help you?"

"No. I don't think so."

"You're sure?"

"Yes. I'll just wait by the fire."

I took a seat next to Sammy. You can always trust a dog to find the best spot in the room. I'd just sat down when the door to Evelyn's office opened.

A man who looked like a member of the grounds crew came walking out with his head lowered. His heavy jacket was unzipped, the flannel shirt beneath it buttoned all the way up to his chin. His boots left damp impressions on the paisley-patterned rug. Evelyn thanked him for his cooperation, then beckoned to me.

Evelyn's office was small and square. It was brightly lit by two wide windows that offered a sparkling view of the mountain outside. One wall held a compact fireplace that was laid, but not currently lit. A row of framed photographs adorned the mantelpiece above it.

A cherrywood desk took up much of the space in the middle of the office. Sheriff Finley was standing behind it. She was a tall, broad-shouldered woman, probably in her late forties. Her stern gaze and no-nonsense stance made me suspect that she'd started at the bottom of the local law enforcement agency and worked her way up to her current position the hard way.

No wonder the man before me had left her presence with his head bowed. I'd just arrived and already I felt intimidated.

Finley's hair was nut-brown shot through with strands of gray. It had been flattened by the uniform hat that was now sitting on the desk beside a large pad of paper where she'd apparently been taking notes. The sheriff stared for a moment, taking my measure. Then she waved me to a straight-backed chair she'd positioned beside the desk.

"You're not a member of the staff," she said as we both sat down.

"No, I'm a guest. My husband and I arrived yesterday. We're here for the holiday event."

"Valentine's Day." Finley didn't bother to hide her disdain.

Message received, I thought. Maybe there was no significant other in the sheriff's life. Maybe she didn't want one. Maybe she didn't even believe in romance. None of that was my problem. Even so, I felt as though I'd already been labeled frivolous and my concerns had been dismissed.

Sheriff Finley took down my name, phone number, and the number of my room. Then she asked how I'd known Belinda Rush.

"We met for the first time yesterday," I told her. "Just after my husband and I checked in. You're probably aware that she was the event coordinator here at the inn."

Finley nodded, encouraging me to continue.

"I barely knew Belinda," I admitted. "But I might know something about her. Was her body found near the ice-skating pond?"

The question earned me a hard look. "Why would you think that?"

"I have a dog and I've been walking her in the area behind the inn. This morning, when I attempted to do so, a deputy told me that the area was off limits."

The sheriff remained silent. It was an effective technique. It made me want to keep talking.

"The thing is, I saw Belinda out there last night when I was exercising Faith."

"Last night?" Suddenly I had her full attention. Finley picked up her pen and pulled the pad closer. "Faith is the dog?"

"Yes."

"What time are we talking about?"

"After the movie ended. Probably around eleven p.m. Sammy was with us too."

"You mean Evelyn's dog?"

"That's right."

She was scribbling hasty notes as I spoke. "Where were you exactly?"

"At first I was just behind the inn. The dogs were loose and they were running around in the snow. I was worried that they were getting too far away, so I started down the path that leads to the skating pond."

"And that's when you saw Belinda?"

"Yes. She was standing near the skate shack. There was a man there with her." I paused, then added, "It looked like they were kissing."

Sheriff Finley's gaze flicked upward. "Who was the man?"

"I don't know. As I said, my husband and I have only been at the inn for less than a day."

"Can you describe him?"

I nodded. "I also saw him earlier in the evening, at the movie. At least six feet tall and handsome. Longish dark brown hair and a bit of a tan. Late thirties, maybe forty. In the activities room, it looked as though he and Belinda were together, but they didn't want anyone else to notice that they were."

Finley had stopped writing. Now she was chewing on the top of her pen. "That's an interesting assessment."

I shrugged.

"Do you think he's an employee here?"

I considered, then said, "That would make sense. He seemed very much at home. Plus, most of the guests here this weekend are visibly coupled up."

"There was a quarter moon last night," the sheriff

said. "It would have been quite dark outside. Are you certain that the man you saw by the pond was the same man you'd seen with Belinda earlier?"

"Reasonably sure. This place is well lit at night. And of course the snow brightens everything."

Finley didn't follow up with another question. Instead she sat in silence for a minute. It felt like a long time.

Finally she said, "So what you're telling me is that you were probably the last person to see Belinda Rush alive."

Startled, I straightened in my seat. "No, that's incorrect," I replied firmly. *And way, way off base.* "The last time I saw Belinda, she and the man were still outside and still together."

The sheriff declined to acknowledge my comment. Instead she busied herself tearing the top sheet off her pad and folding it into a small square. I took that to mean she thought our conversation was finished.

I still had questions of my own, however.

"Don't you find Belinda's death suspicious?" I asked. "How could a young, healthy woman die of exposure only a short distance away from the building where she lived and worked? Why was she out there in the first place? The man she was with must have come back inside, so why didn't Belinda?"

Sheriff Finley folded her hands together on top of

the desk. I saw that her nails were bitten short. It was the only flaw in her otherwise pristine appearance.

"Those are all good questions," she allowed. "But let's not get ahead of ourselves. Right now, all we know for certain is that Belinda Rush expired at some point during the night. It's entirely possible she died of natural causes. We'll have more facts once the medical examiner has had a chance to prepare his report. Then, if we need to, we'll go looking for answers."

By the time the report was available, the holiday weekend would probably be over, I realized. The inn would have emptied, its guests returning to homes in as many as five adjoining states. Sam had been right when he'd pointed out that an investigation would be bad for business. Both for the White Birch Inn, and for the small town of Steepleton in which it was located.

I stood up and walked to the door. "I'm sorry if I wasted your time."

Sheriff Finley offered me an enigmatic smile. "It's not a problem," she said.

Chapter
Six

That hadn't gone the way I'd thought it would.

I strode out of the office and headed toward the stairs. Evelyn glanced up as I went by. She looked as though she hoped I would stop to talk, but I ignored the implied invitation and kept walking. After my conversation with Sheriff Finley I wasn't in a chatty mood.

When I got back to the room, Bertie and Frank were still there with Sam. Seeing the expression on my face, none of them said a word. Faith jumped off the bed and came running over. I knelt down and wrapped my arms around her neck. It only took a few seconds of dog therapy before I began to feel better.

I sat down cross-legged on the floor and pulled Faith into my lap. "So," I said. "I guess we missed breakfast?"

"Don't change the subject," Sam told me.

"What subject? I just got here. And when I'm annoyed, I get hungry."

"Now we have two subjects," Sam said. "First, what did you need to talk to Sheriff Finley about? And second, why did your conversation with her annoy you?"

Frank was popping chocolates in his mouth from an open, heart-shaped box on the table. He stopped and raised his hand. "I know! It's because you said something dumb to the lady sheriff, isn't it?"

"That's *woman* sheriff to you." Bertie clasped his hand and pulled it down. Then she reached over and closed the candy box. "And don't insult your sister. Melanie almost never says dumb things."

"Says you," Frank retorted. "You didn't grow up with her."

I had no intention of squabbling with Frank like we were still children. Instead I said, "Last night after the movie, when I was outside with Faith, I saw Belinda out near the skating shack with a man."

Sam frowned. "You didn't say anything about that when you got back."

I cocked a brow in his direction. "When I got back, you were stepping out of the shower and, as I recall, we found something much more interesting to do than talk."

"Oh," he said.

Oh indeed. "That's why I wanted to talk to Sheriff Finley."

"What did she think of that?" Sam asked.

"For one thing, she said it meant I was the last person to see Belinda Rush alive." Even just repeating that made me feel grumpy again. I slid my fingers under Faith's chin. As I scratched one of her favorite spots, she wriggled happily in my arms. That helped.

"No, you weren't," said Bertie. She was no dumb bunny.

"That's what I told the sheriff. Besides, I just met Belinda yesterday. What possible reason could I have for wanting her dead?"

"I can come up with a few ideas," Frank said. "Maybe Belinda neglected to sign you up for couples' crocheting."

I looked at Bertie. "Is that a thing?"

She shook her head.

"Couples' canoeing," Frank tried again.

"Still nope," said Bertie.

"How about couples' canoodling?"

"As long as Sam's onboard, I don't need anyone's permission for that." I smiled his way, but Sam wasn't about to be sidetracked.

"So what you're saying is that you suspect there was foul play," he said.

I nodded. "Don't you?"

"You *always* suspect foul play," Bertie pointed out. "And unfortunately I'm usually right."

After that conversation, we were all ready for a change of scenery. Literally. What was the point of visiting a resort in the beautiful Berkshire Mountains and staying inside our rooms?

We checked the schedule of activities that had been delivered to our rooms the previous evening. This morning, we'd all signed up to go tobogganing. That sounded like the perfect way to clear our heads and reset the day.

Within minutes, we'd pulled on sweaters and boots, wrapped knitted scarves around our necks, and shoved warm, woolly gloves into the pockets of our parkas. Watching us suit up, Faith danced around the room in anticipation. She could tell something fun was about to happen.

On the way outside, I detoured our group past the dining room. To our delight, we found a buffet table stocked with portable breakfast items for those who'd missed the morning meal. I took a cinnamon bun. Sam and Frank grabbed energy bars. Bertie made do with an apple. Faith, who'd had her own breakfast earlier, could share mine.

The lower slope of the mountain wasn't long enough

for skiing, but it was just the right size for sledding. The snow on the wide tobogganing track was packed down hard, slick in the middle and icy on the sides. Previous sledders had tamped down a trail beside the track that we could use to climb to the top of the incline.

Half a dozen sleek wooden toboggans were standing on end, leaning against the back wall of the inn. Each had a curved front with tow rope attached, and plenty of room for passengers on its long, flat-bottomed base behind. A sign above the sleds invited us to help ourselves and recommended that children wear helmets and only ride with their parents.

Frank chose a sled from the end of the row, lowered it to the snowy ground, and stared at it as if he knew enough about the sport to be assessing the equipment's virtues. None of us were fooled.

"Do we want one toboggan or two?" he asked.

"Two," I guessed. I was hardly an expert either. "One for each couple?"

"One is more fun," said Bertie.

"How come?" asked Sam.

"The heavier the weight on the sled, the faster you fly down the hill. Plus, the best way to do it is for everyone to cuddle up next to each other and hold on to the legs of the person behind you. That way nobody falls off."

"That sounds cozy," I said. "And perfect for the theme of the weekend. Let's give it a try."

Faith followed us up the hill, leaping from drift to drift and tunneling through the snow with her nose. By the time we reached the top of the slope, her face and ears were sparkling with droplets of ice.

The temperature was around freezing, but fortunately there was no wind. The sun was shining in a cloudless blue sky. It was a beautiful day to be on the mountain. Clearly we weren't the only people who'd thought so. We waited in line behind four other groups for our turn to tackle the slope.

Some couples made it all the way to the bottom. Others skidded on the ice and overturned partway down the hill. No matter the outcome, everyone was laughing and having a good time. It appeared that the sad news Evelyn had delivered earlier wasn't spoiling anyone's enjoyment of the day.

The first time our toboggan went flying down the mountain, Faith came racing after us, barking joyfully. After a second trip back up the side of the slope, however, she was looking a bit winded. Faith was fit for her age, but this was more exercise than she'd had in a while.

For our second run I put her on my lap, wedged in between Sam and me. Faith didn't love that idea. She squirmed most of the way down the hill—I knew because I was holding her tight. At the bottom I decided not to try that again.

"Faith needs a chance to catch her breath. She and I are going to sit the next one out," I said to the rest of the gang when we'd finished disentangling ourselves.

Sam had already grabbed the tow rope to drag the toboggan back up the hill. He turned around, surprised. "Is everything okay?"

"It's fine," I said. "Faith and I are just taking a short breather. Go have fun and we'll watch from here."

I doubted anyone was fooled by that excuse, but Sam and Bertie were dog lovers too. They could see that it was in Faith's best interest not to have to scramble right back up the slippery slope.

"We'll be right back," Sam told Faith. "Try not to let her get in too much trouble while we're gone."

The Poodle answered him with a cheerful woof.

There was a wooden bench nearby, situated to offer an optimal view of the mountain. I sat down and Faith hopped up beside me. The midday sun, reflecting off both the snow and the white building behind us, warmed us from both sides.

I unzipped the top of my jacket, then took off my gloves and stuffed them in my pockets. When Faith lay down with her head in my lap, I tilted my face up toward the golden rays and closed my eyes.

"Melanie Travis," said a deep voice. "That's you, right?"

I opened my eyes too quickly. I'd been facing the sun, so for a moment I saw nothing but spots dancing across my field of vision. Silhouetted just behind them was the shadowy figure of a man.

I blinked quickly several times. It didn't help much. My hand was resting on Faith's withers. I felt her stiffen, then sit up. I wondered what she was able to see that I wasn't.

"Yes, that's me," I said. "Is there a problem?"

"You bet there is."

Finally my vision cleared and I realized I was looking up at the man whom I'd seen with Belinda the previous night. From this vantage point he looked taller than I remembered. He had even features and a slightly square jaw. His eyebrows were drawn downward over a pair of piercing brown eyes. For a man, he had beautiful lips. Which was probably not what I needed to be focusing on right at the moment.

"Excuse me," I said, standing up. "Who are you?"

"Cliff Granger." He didn't offer his hand. Neither did I.

"Do you work here?"

"Lifeguard." The man gestured toward a domed, glass-enclosed wing that was attached to the side of the inn. "And you're a guest. I checked on that. You just got here yesterday. So I have no idea why you felt the need to meddle in something that's none of your business."

"Meddle," I said.

His head dipped in a short, sharp nod. "It's bad enough what happened."

Beside me, Faith was staring at the man and muttering unhappily under her breath. I placed a hand on her back, willing her to relax. I wanted to hear what Cliff Granger had to say.

He eyed my big black dog and took a step back. "But then you had to *volunteer* to talk to the sheriff—and whatever you told her made me look like a suspect in Belinda's death."

"Suspect?" I repeated innocently. "Evelyn said it was an accident."

"Evelyn has it right," he snapped. "But that doesn't mean there aren't questions."

Abruptly I realized something. "Who told you what I said to Sheriff Finley?" I doubted that the sheriff would have released that information.

"It doesn't matter." Cliff snorted. "The fact is, I know it was you."

"I only told her what I saw," I said mildly.

"Which was what?"

"You and Belinda outside last night by the skating shack."

"So? What's it to you?"

"Absolutely nothing," I replied. "Until Belinda's body was discovered near there this morning."

"I didn't have anything to do with that," Cliff growled. "Belinda was fine the last time I saw her."

"When was that?"

Cliff looked over his shoulder in both directions. No one was near enough to hear what we were saying. Nevertheless, he lowered his voice.

"Yeah, she and I were out there. But then she said she had to go meet someone. I escorted her back inside the inn and we parted at the door."

"Who was she meeting?" I asked.

"How would I know?"

Considering that it had been late at night, and that Belinda was a woman with whom he had a relationship, it seemed odd to me that Cliff wouldn't have been curious about that. *If* he was telling the truth.

"And you told that to Sheriff Finley?"

"Of course I did. But that doesn't mean she believed me. My name would never have even been in her head if you hadn't put it there. So this is on you."

Not really, I thought. Because I wasn't the one who'd been with Belinda the night before.

"If you and she came back inside the inn together, why did she go out again?"

"I'm telling you, I don't know. I have no idea where Belinda went or what she did after I left her at the back of the lobby."

"Then it sounds as though you don't have anything to worry about," I said. "Except maybe that you and Belinda were sneaking around and keeping your relationship a secret?"

"Again," he ground out. "That's none of your damn business."

"Had you been seeing each other long?"

"Long enough."

I frowned. "That sounds ominous."

"Lady, you'd better stop putting words in my mouth. It's company policy, okay? Employees aren't allowed to fraternize with guests or other employees."

The White Birch Inn was a fairly large resort, but it was still a close community. I suspected it would only have been a matter of time before Belinda and Cliff were found out.

"What would happen if you got caught?" I asked. "Would your relationship with Belinda have cost you your job?"

"I didn't even want to know. That's why I took Belinda outside last night. I knew I needed to break up with her."

"That was an interesting way to end a relationship," I said. "One last kiss?"

Cliff leaned down until his face was only inches from mine. Faith's lips fluttered in a low growl. As usual, my Poodle and I were on the same wavelength. I wanted to growl myself.

"Stay the hell out of my life," he snapped. "Or I'll make sure you'll regret it."

Chapter
Seven

"What's going on here?"

Suddenly Sam was standing beside us. Faith looked just as happy about that development as I was. The hair on the ruff of her neck had been standing up. Now it settled back down into place. Sam was so close to Cliff that their shoulders were nearly touching. He ignored the other man and looked only at me.

"This is Cliff Granger," I said. "He's the inn's life-guard. He was just leaving."

"Lifeguard?" Sam eyed the man up and down. "In that case, you're a long way from where you ought to be."

"Right." Cliff smirked. He spun on his heel and strode away.

Sam watched him go. Behind Sam, I could see Bertie and Frank standing at the bottom of the slope with the toboggan. They were waiting to see what would happen next. Come to think of it, so was I. When Cliff was gone, Sam turned and waved to them.

"I'm going to sit this one out too," he called. "Mel and I will catch up with you next time."

I sat back down on the bench. Sam pulled off his gloves and sat beside me. Faith hopped down and went to investigate a nearby tree.

"What was that about?" he asked. "Who's Cliff Granger and what made him think it was okay for him to get in your face like that?"

"It turns out he's the guy I saw last night with Belinda."

Judging by the expression on Sam's face, he didn't like the sound of that. "You mean just before she died?"

I nodded. "He said he didn't do it."

"Of course he did."

"He said he walked her back to the inn and they parted at the door. Belinda told him there was someone she needed to go see."

"In the middle of the night?" Sam sounded skeptical.

I shrugged. I wasn't about to defend a story that didn't make sense to me either. "Cliff was angry that I spoke with the sheriff. He said I made him look suspicious."

"It seems to me he did that to himself. That guy appears to have a temper. I'm thinking you ought to steer clear of him."

"I agree," I said. When I snapped my fingers, Faith looked up. I beckoned her back to my side. "Now that I know who Cliff is and where he works, I'll make every effort to be elsewhere."

A sudden screech rent the air. It came from the direction of the slope. Sam and I both turned to look. Without our steadying presence, the toboggan—with Bertie and Frank on it—was careening from side to side as it hurtled down the hill.

Frank was supposed to be steering. His face was white beneath his knit cap. Bertie, sitting behind him with her arms wrapped around his body, was screaming with laughter. Moments later, the sled tipped over and they both spilled out. Their momentum sent them sliding down the remainder of the toboggan track in a dizzying spin.

Sam and I jumped up and ran over to help. Faith reached the snow-covered couple first. Bertie was rolling on the ground. To my relief, she was still laughing.

"That was great," she chortled.

"Speak for yourself," Frank grumbled as they stood up and brushed themselves off. "I think I just saw my life flash before my eyes."

"Is that why you didn't bother steering the sled?" I asked.

When Frank flicked a glance in my direction, then stooped down to the ground, I knew what was coming. Immediately I followed suit. It took me less time to pack together a snowball than it did him.

As my brother straightened and raised his arm, I let fly. Before he even realized what was happening, my snowball had hit him squarely in the chest. His snowball passed harmlessly over my head.

"Hey!" cried Frank. "No fair."

"Good luck making that case," Sam said with a chuckle. He walked over to retrieve our errant toboggan from one of the attendants. "I think we've had enough sledding for one day. Is anyone else ready for a hot toddy?"

"Me!" That sounded like a great idea. Faith would be able to join us on the bar's outdoor terrace. And I'd be able to think about something other than my curious encounter with Cliff Granger.

After lunch, Bertie decided that she and I were going gift shopping in the ballroom. "This will get you in the holiday mood," she said.

Little did she know. If Sam and I devoted any more time to celebrating Valentine's Day we'd never make it out of bed.

It turned out, however, that Sam was happy to ditch me for the afternoon. Improbably, Frank had signed the two of them up for an archery competition. It was slated to be held in the field behind the inn. The sheriff's and the coroner's vehicles had left by late morning, and the space was once again open for guests to enjoy.

"Archery?" I said to my brother as we all paused in the lobby before heading in different directions. "When was the last time you shot a bow and arrow?"

"Umm . . ." Frank thought back. "Maybe never?"

"So what made you think it would be a good idea now?"

He shrugged. "It was on the schedule and I thought it looked like fun. Besides, how hard can it be?"

"To master a sport that you've never previously attempted well enough in one afternoon to win a contest?" Bertie laughed. "I'm thinking pretty much impossible." She leaned over and gave her husband a kiss. "But that's what I love about you, honey."

"That he's impossible?" I asked.

"No, that he keeps life interesting. There's never a dull moment with Frank around."

"Hmm," said Sam. "That sounds familiar. Sometimes I feel the same way about Melanie. Maybe that trait runs in their family?"

I looked at him. "When Bertie said that about Frank it sounded more complimentary. I thought you enjoyed my little peccadillos."

"It *was* complimentary about me." Frank preened. "But the jury's still out on you. And pecca-*whats*?"

I reached over and patted my brother's shoulder. "Sometimes it's easy to tell that you make sandwiches for a living."

Frank was actually co-owner of a successful coffee bar and café back home, but right at the moment I didn't feel the need to split hairs.

"Hey!" Now he sounded wounded. "Don't forget about the Christmas tree farm."

"As if." Bertie snorted. During the previous holiday season, she and I had both been pressed into service behind the counter of that venture.

Sam cleared his throat. "Frankly, the idea of archery is beginning to sound a whole lot better than listening to this. Frank, let's go get our gear. I'll meet you out back in ten minutes."

"I'll be right back," I said to Bertie. "I'm just going to run up and get Faith." The Poodle had been snoozing in our room while we ate lunch.

"Take your time." Bertie was already heading across the lobby to say hello to Sammy. She dropped onto a love seat and called the dog to her. "I'm going to let this big fluffy boy keep me company."

A short while later Faith was by my side when Bertie and I opened the double doors that led to the ballroom. I paused in the doorway to get my bearings, then quickly realized there was so much to see that it was hard to decide which direction to look first.

The huge space before us was a riotous profusion of colors, sights, and sounds. Garlands made of red and pink ribbons were strung across the walls. Sparkling decorations featuring hearts and cupids adorned nearly every surface. Even the air smelled wonderful.

Speakers in the corners of the ceiling piped music into the room. Currently, Frank Sinatra was crooning a love song. The singer was barely audible, however, over the babble of conversation generated by several dozen enthusiastic shoppers browsing at the numerous booths set up around the large room.

Most of them appeared to be women. I wondered if the archery competition was a bigger draw than I'd suspected, and all the men were outside with bows and arrows.

I glanced down at Faith and realized that she had her ears flattened against her head. Maybe she wasn't a Sinatra fan. When I gave her a reassuring pat, she pressed her body against my leg. Crowds can be tough for dogs, but as long as Faith was with me, she didn't have to worry.

"This place is amazing," I said to Bertie.

"I know. Right? Frank and I stopped by briefly yesterday afternoon and my wish list is already half a page long. What are you hoping Sam gets you for Valentine's Day?"

"Actually, I haven't given it any thought. I figured this trip was our present to each other."

"Pffft." Bertie blew out a breath. "You can do better than that. Don't you want to celebrate the most romantic day of the year in style?"

"Sam and I celebrate our romance every day."

Bertie laughed out loud. "Said no married woman *ever*. Especially not one with children."

I laughed with her. "Okay, but it sounded good, didn't it?"

"For about ten seconds. Now let's get real. Roses? Truffles? Maybe a pair of earrings? What's your secret wish?"

Aside from a night of totally uninterrupted sleep, I had no idea. So I turned the question back on her. "You've clearly given this some thought. What's at the top of your list?"

"Step this way," said Bertie, "and I'll give you the grand tour."

She wasn't kidding. The tour Bertie and I took around the ballroom wasn't just grand, it was an exercise in extravagance. We sniffed French-milled soap, sampled decadent buttercream fudge, sipped a vintage cabernet, and draped strands of lustrous pearls around our necks.

The jeweler was particularly insistent that his wares were the best in the room. Of course they were also the most expensive. He didn't mention that part.

Instead he gestured dismissively toward another jewelry shop across the way.

"Only silver and semiprecious stones," he scoffed. "And the proprietor has the nerve to resent *me* for being here. As if her paltry baubles are even in the same class as my lovely jewels."

Bertie and I shared a look. She'd heard something similar the day before.

"Did you know there were going to be two jewelry shops here when you agreed to come for the weekend?" I asked him.

"Certainly not. I was told to expect there to be about a dozen vendors. Instead there are twice that many. And now all of us are stuffed in here side by side like sardines in a can."

"Who handled your booking for the event?"

Abruptly his face fell. "It was the unfortunate woman who lost her life last night. And now that I remember that, I take back everything I said. It's not my place to speak ill of the dead."

Bertie and I unclasped the pearls and handed them back. The jeweler laid the two strands reverently on a black velvet cloth where they would show to their best advantage. Then he picked up two business cards from a stack on the counter and handed one to each of us.

"For your husbands," he said, then winked. "Or boyfriends?"

Bertie and I both laughed. "Husbands," we said.

The man gave Faith a friendly pat on the head and then we were on our way. This time we didn't get far.

"Oh my god," a woman squealed. "That's the biggest Poodle I ever seen!"

She and another woman halted abruptly in front of us. Both of them were in their twenties and looked as though they were ready to audition for *Real Housewives of the Berkshires*. Their hair and makeup were perfect. While Bertie and I were dressed in casual slacks and wool sweaters, they had on chic designer après ski wear.

The two women had their hands filled with packages. It looked as though they'd already bought plenty of gifts for themselves.

Faith gazed up at the two of them and wagged her tail obligingly.

"Her name is Faith," I said. "And she likes making new friends, so feel free to say hello to her. I'm Melanie and this is Bertie."

"Molly and Trina." The woman who'd spoken to us pointed first to herself, then to her companion.

"That's not just a regular Poodle," Trina said authoritatively. "That's a *royal* Standard."

Bertie and I looked at each other. The AKC recognizes three varieties of Poodles: Toy, Miniature, and Standard. The term *royal Standard* came about as a marketing tool for crafty breeders to convince buyers that their dogs were bigger and better than other Standard Poodles.

"No, Faith is a regular Standard Poodle," I told her.

"I don't *think* so." Trina was very sure of that. "You should call the person you got her from and ask."

The notion of me asking Aunt Peg if she was breeding royal Standard Poodles made me sputter out a laugh. Bertie looked similarly amused. She and I were about to move on when Molly suddenly reached out and grabbed my arm.

"Wait a minute!" she cried. "I know who you are. You're the woman who saw what happened to Belinda."

Chapter
Eight

Yikes! Where had that idea come from? Was there a witness who'd come forward? If so, it was news to me.

"No," I said, gently withdrawing my arm. "You must have me confused with someone else."

"No." Molly shook her head. "I saw you. I was passing through the lobby when you went in and talked to the sheriff. None of the other guests did that. One of the bellhops said you must know something important."

She leaned in close as though we were coconspirators. A silky tendril of hair fell forward across her face. I was pretty sure Molly had extensions. "So what really happened? You can tell us. Trina and I are good at keeping secrets."

"I don't have any secrets," I said. Well, none that I was going to share with these two. "Yes, I did speak with Sheriff Finley this morning. But I have no idea why Belinda died."

"Well, that's disappointing." Molly drew back. "I wanted to call Sean and tell him what happened."

"Who's Sean?"

"Belinda's ex-boyfriend," Trina said.

More news. Suddenly it occurred to me that we might want to continue this conversation in a less busy and more private place.

Bertie must have read my mind. "Melanie and I were about to go to the lounge for a drink. Would you ladies like to join us?"

"I hope you're talking about something alcoholic," said Molly. "All this shopping has left me parched. You can lead the way."

Our small procession—four women, a Poodle, and enough bags and bundles to fill a minivan—made our way across the hall to a cozy lounge beside the bar at the rear of the building. This time of day, with both indoor and outdoor activities in progress, the wood-paneled room was empty. That suited my purposes perfectly.

We hadn't even sat down before an attentive waiter appeared to take our drink order. Bertie and I chose hot chocolate. Molly asked for a dirty martini with two olives. Trina ordered a margarita with extra salt.

The drinks arrived within minutes. By then, we'd settled in a group of tartan armchairs near a picture window. It was framed by brocade curtains the color of cranberries, and our view overlooked the skating pond.

The waiter delivered our order, then handed me a supersized dog biscuit for Faith. I looked at him in surprise.

"I won't tell Sammy if you won't," he whispered.

"Thank you. Faith will love that." I passed the treat to her, and she lay down beside my chair with the biscuit balanced upright between her front paws.

I waited until Trina and Molly had both had a chance to sample their drinks, then said, "It sounds as though you two knew Belinda before you came here?"

Molly nodded. "We all went to the same college. I guess you'd say we were more acquaintances than friends. After we got out, we mostly stayed in touch through social media. Trina and I both got jobs in Albany."

"What about Belinda?" Bertie asked. "Where did she go?"

Molly and Trina appeared to share some unspoken communication. "Belinda bounced around a bit," Trina said carefully.

"She had a hard time finding a job she thought was a good fit," Molly added.

My cocoa was warm and delicious. It left a foamy mustache above the rim of my lip. I licked it off and said, "How long had Belinda been working here at the inn?"

"I'm not sure. Maybe since last summer?" Molly took another sip of her martini. "It seemed like she was happy here, so that was good."

"Where does Sean fit in?" I said.

"He went to the same school as us. Plus, he works in Albany now too. He and Belinda used to be together, but I guess she didn't like the idea of a long distance relationship."

"What brought you here this weekend?" Bertie asked.

"That was Belinda's doing," Trina told us. "The Valentine's Day event was her idea and she wanted it to be successful. She said that if we came, she could get us a deal on our room."

"The inn seems pretty full," I said.

"Yeah, but that's not always the case," Molly replied. "Belinda said some months they struggle to get bookings. Maybe she was worried about keeping her job. Anyway, her boss said 'fill the rooms,' so she did."

I took another sip of my cocoa and felt sorry for the woman who'd lost her life overnight. Even though they weren't close, I'd have expected Molly and Trina to be more affected by Belinda's death. Instead, after they'd heard the news, they'd gone shopping. I was having a hard time wrapping my head around that.

"If you don't mind my saying so," I commented,

"neither of you seems very upset about what happened."

"Don't get me wrong," Molly said. "It was definitely a shock, hearing that Belinda died."

Beside her, Trina nodded. She signaled the waiter for another margarita.

"But Bel was a bit of a thrill seeker, always on the lookout for her next adventure. She dropped out of college after junior year and set off to see the world— or as much of it as she could afford. We drifted apart because our lives had nothing in common anymore."

Trina nodded again. "Belinda liked testing herself. If she'd died of exposure on top of Mount McKinley, I wouldn't have been surprised. But here? Yeah, that was unexpected. And extremely unfortunate. But there's nothing Molly and I can do about it. We came here because Belinda wanted us to have a good time. So that's what we're trying to do."

Trina and Molly spent the next half hour unwrapping their purchases and showing them off. They'd bought perfume, wine, scented candles, matching silk lingerie, and pillows on which their names had been embroidered inside a red and gold heart.

Bertie and I were meant to be dazzled and we did our best to give that impression. Having finished her biscuit, Faith settled her muzzle between her paws and slept through the entire show. I wouldn't have minded doing the same.

When Molly and Trina ordered their third round of drinks, Bertie and I excused ourselves. Faith hopped up and followed us out.

"I'm not sure about those two," Bertie said under her breath.

"Me either. Do you think we heard the real reason Belinda invited them here for the weekend?"

"I have no idea. But one thing's certain. She didn't intend to end up dead in a snow drift while they were here."

We'd reached the foot of the staircase in the lobby when Evelyn stuck her head out of her office. "Melanie, do you have a minute? There's something I'd like to ask you."

I glanced at Bertie. "Do you mind taking Faith upstairs with you?"

"Easy peasy," she replied.

Evelyn stepped aside as I entered the office, then closed the door behind us. The straight-backed chair I'd sat in earlier was nowhere to be seen. Space was at a premium in the small room. Now there was only one place to sit—the chair behind the desk. Evelyn ignored it and we both remained standing.

Now that I was here, she seemed reluctant to speak. When we'd met the previous afternoon, the inn's owner had been poised and gracious, secure in her position as lady of the manor. The day's events had clearly taken their toll, however.

Evelyn looked tired. Wisps of hair had escaped from her chignon and her lipstick was partially bitten away. "This is awkward," she said with a small laugh. "I realize we barely know each other"—she paused to clear her throat—"but I'd like to ask a favor of you."

"Go on," I said. Her reluctance fostered my own.

"I understand you possess a skill for solving mysteries."

That wasn't at all what I'd expected. "Where did you hear that?"

"I spoke with the other woman in your group earlier."

"Bertie," I said. That must have been after lunch when I'd run upstairs to get Faith.

Evelyn nodded. "She told me you'd been involved in several police investigations."

"I just ask questions," I said. "People say all sorts of interesting things in the course of a conversation. I'm good at gathering information and putting the pieces together."

"Clues, you mean."

"Sometimes." I intended to remain noncommittal until Evelyn explained herself.

She walked over to her desk and picked up an oval

glass paperweight. For a minute, she simply stood and turned it end over end in her palm. She appeared to be mulling something over.

I gazed out the window and waited in silence. I was pretty sure where this conversation was headed, but I wasn't about to prod it in that direction.

"Chats and observations," Evelyn finally said. "That doesn't sound like too much to ask. Here at the inn, it's not unusual for guests and staff to interact and get to know one another."

She glanced my way with a small smile. "If you were discreet, no one would suspect anything. Indeed, it appears that you've already stumbled over something since you requested a meeting with Sheriff Finley."

I drew my gaze away from the view. "Did she tell you what we talked about?"

"She did not." Evelyn paused, in case I wanted to fill her in. When I remained silent, she said, "The White Birch Inn has been in my family for three generations. So it's to be expected that I have a proprietary interest in everything that happens here."

I nodded.

"Perhaps you could coordinate your efforts with those of the sheriff."

Suddenly it all made sense. Evelyn wasn't just hoping that I could beat Sheriff Finley to the resolution of their mutual problem—she also wanted me to provide her with inside information about the sheriff's investigation.

"Let me be clear," I said. "You're asking me to seek out answers with regard to Belinda's death—while law enforcement does the same—in order to insure that any *proprietary* information reaches you first?"

Evelyn frowned. She hadn't expected me to be so blunt. "Naturally I want this tragic event resolved and put behind us as quickly as possible. But at the same time, it's of the utmost importance that the White Birch Inn be found blameless in what transpired."

So now we knew where we both stood. Obviously Evelyn had a vested interest in the outcome of the investigation. And there was no point in denying that I was curious.

"I suppose I could ask a few questions," I told her.

"Good." She walked around behind her desk and pulled out the chair. "Then that's settled."

"Starting with you," I said.

"Oh?" She hadn't expected that.

"How well did you know Belinda?"

She swished the skirt of her dress to one side and sat down. "Not at all, really. I was her employer."

Noted. In case I hadn't understood the first time, Evelyn was reiterating that she intended for me to snoop around while she remained firmly on the sidelines.

"Still, you might have some idea who her friends were among the staff. Who did she hang out with on her days off?"

Evelyn stopped to think. "Catelyn Hughes. She works in the spa. And Jill Lively is our head of hospitality. Those girls are all around the same age. The inn's attic was converted to staff quarters years ago. I seem to recall that their rooms are next to each other."

I committed the two names to memory. I also noted that she hadn't mentioned Cliff Granger. "Anyone else?"

"Not that I can recall." The paperweight Evelyn was holding slipped from her hand. The glass orb landed on her desk with a sharp crack.

That was going to leave a mark.

Her lips pursed in annoyance. "I need to get back to work. Is that all?"

"Just one more question," I said. "A few minutes ago you asked what I talked about with Sheriff Finley."

"Yes."

"I told her that on the night Belinda died, I saw her outside near the skating shack with Cliff Granger." I didn't mention their embrace. Evelyn would have seen that for herself. "Did you also tell her that?"

"No." Evelyn looked puzzled. "Why would I?"

"Because you saw them too."

She opened her laptop and pulled it toward her. Clearly I was being dismissed. "I have no idea what you're talking about," she said firmly. "I was inside the inn all night. I didn't see a thing."

Chapter
Nine

Back in the lobby, I pulled out my phone and called Sam. He didn't pick up. He and Frank were probably still outside shooting arrows. It seemed as though the competition had been going on for a while. Maybe it was taking so long because they were winning.

Yeah, right.

I tried Bertie next. "I'm guessing the guys aren't back yet?"

"Nope. It's just me and Faith up here. We're good. I'm sitting here with my feet up, eating dark chocolate and watching daytime TV. I never get to do that at home."

"No chocolate for Faith," I said.

"Of course not." We both knew how dangerous chocolate was for dogs. "Faith is taking a well-earned nap. For an old dog, she's had a busy day."

"I know. Thanks for taking care of her." I sank

down in a nearby chair. "Did you tell Evelyn I should get involved in Sheriff Finley's investigation?"

There was a pause before Bertie replied. "I might have mentioned something about your past exploits."

"Now she wants my help," I said.

"Good."

"Good?" I echoed. "I'm supposed to be on vacation."

"That doesn't mean you're going to stop using your brain." Bertie sounded pleased with herself. "Besides, I know you. There's no way you weren't going to get involved. So now your snoopiness is sanctioned."

"Snoopiness?"

"Yeah." Even though I couldn't see her, I could tell she was grinning. "You know. Like the dog in the cartoon strip."

I hung up on her. I thought that made a fitting statement, until I realized I still had another thing to say.

Bertie picked up on the first ring. "You again?"

"There's someone else I need to see," I told her. "Are you good with Faith for another twenty minutes?"

"Sure. No prob. Kelly Clarkson's about to sing her new song. Gotta go."

This time she hung up on me. I suppose I deserved that.

The spa was located on the lower level. That was all I knew about it. A binder in my room listed all the services that were available at the resort, but so far I hadn't bothered to check it out. I had no idea what kinds of treatments could be booked and what Catelyn Hughes's job might be. Hopefully she could spare a few minutes to talk to me.

The spa's reception area was decorated in soothing hues of light blue and cream. A woman dressed in a matching smock was seated behind a low counter. She greeted me with a cheerful smile.

"I'm here to see Catelyn Hughes," I said.

"Do you have an appointment for a Swedish massage?" Her gaze went to a nearby computer screen.

"No, I don't. Do I need one?"

"Let me see." The receptionist glanced up and smiled. "You're in luck. It looks like Catelyn can fit you in. Can I have your name and room number?"

I gave it to her. She typed it in, then said, "If you wouldn't mind having a seat for just a moment, I'll go get her for you."

The woman disappeared through a door in the back wall. A short time later, a different woman emerged. She was petite and curvy, with straight blond hair that was cut in an asymmetrical chin length bob. Her smock was powder blue and her name was embroidered over her heart.

"Ms. Travis?" she said. "If you could come with me?"

"I don't have time for a massage," I said as I followed her to a private room. "I was actually hoping I could ask you a few questions."

The space held a padded massage table with several folded towels on top of it. In one corner of the room was a screened-off area where I was meant to undress. Just inside the door I saw a small table with a chair on either side of it. Catelyn motioned me to one of the chairs. She took the seat opposite me.

"Questions?" she said. "About what?"

"I'd like to talk to you about Belinda Rush. I understand that you and she were friends and I'm sorry for your loss."

"Thank you." Catelyn pulled in a breath, then slowly released it. "It's been a hard day. Mrs. Barker gathered all the employees together this morning and told us it was vital that we carry on as usual so that the inn's guests remain comfortable. I'm trying to do that, but it isn't easy. I just can't understand what happened."

"Neither can I," I said. "That's why I wanted to talk to you."

Catelyn considered that. Then she held out her hand across the table and beckoned for me to extend mine. "You're already booked in, so we need to do *something.* If you don't want a full body massage, how about one for your hands?"

I hadn't had a manicure in months. My nails were filed square across and unpainted. But my hands were usually busy and I didn't spend much time worrying about them. As long as Catelyn wasn't horrified by their condition, a hand massage would give us a perfect excuse to spend some time together.

"Sure," I said. "That would be great."

Catelyn took my right hand in hers. She examined it top and bottom, then reached for a tube of lotion. "Coconut oil," she said. "Your nails are in good shape, probably because you don't polish them, but your cuticles are dry." She sandwiched my hand between both of hers and applied the lotion to the back of my hand and fingers in strong, smooth strokes.

Mmmm, that felt good. Why had I never done this before now?

I waited until Catelyn had settled in to a rhythm, then asked, "How well did you know Belinda?"

"Maybe not as well as I thought," she said slowly. "You know . . . considering."

I nodded.

"We met last summer when she came to work here. Sometimes we hung out together when we were both off duty. But her idea of a good time and mine didn't match up at all."

"What do you mean?"

"When I get off work, I want to go somewhere fun. Party, you know? Maybe a bar, or some place with music. Not that there are a lot of entertainment opportunities in a small town like this, but you gotta at least try. Right?"

"Sure." I smiled.

"Belinda . . . she'd have one drink and then she was ready to come back to the inn. I'd be feeding coins into the jukebox and looking around for some guy to dance with and she'd already have one foot out the door."

Maybe that was because Belinda already had a dance partner, I thought.

That led me to my next question. "Do you know what she might have been doing outside the inn late last night?" Obviously I had my own thoughts about that. But I wanted to hear what Catelyn might say.

She glanced up sharply, then lowered her gaze back to our joined hands. "Sorry, I have no idea."

I didn't entirely believe that. Especially since Catelyn was now refusing to look at me. Like maybe she had something to hide. She was still working on my first hand, however, and that meant I had time. I wasn't ready to give up yet.

Catelyn flipped my hand over, then squeezed out another dab of coconut oil. The tips of her fingers massaged my palm. For a moment, I closed my eyes and simply enjoyed the sensation. Then I made myself get back to work.

"Do you think maybe Belinda wasn't interested in going bar hopping with you because she already had a boyfriend?"

"You mean that guy Sean?"

That was unexpected.

"Sure," I said. "Sean. What do you know about him?"

"Belinda said he was old news. Just some guy she used to hang out with in college. He'd gotten some dumb job in law enforcement and she wasn't impressed by that. I don't think they were in touch much anymore. If I had to guess, I'd say Belinda was more into older guys."

"Anyone in particular?" I asked.

Catelyn thought about that as she gently placed my right hand down on the table between us. She then picked up my left hand and repeated the process.

"Look," she said. "You didn't hear this from me."

"Of course not."

"She had her eye on this guy Cliff, who's the lifeguard here. Not that it seemed to be going anywhere. When it comes to fooling around, Cliff pretty much has his choice of the ladies. Belinda told me he wasn't returning her interest."

That certainly wasn't what it had looked like to me.

"And there's another guy, Harley Jones." She rolled her eyes. "I don't understand what she saw in him."

"Who's he?"

"Harley works on the grounds crew. You know, mowing, landscaping, shoveling snow? Talk about a dead-end job."

"Maybe he's a nice person," I said.

"Not nice enough to overcome the fact that he works outside all day with his hands." Catelyn smirked. "I'm guessing there isn't much brain power there. Belinda could have done much better."

Even so, that still made him someone I'd want to talk to. Maybe Harley had wanted Belinda, and Belinda had wanted Cliff. She wouldn't be the first woman to come to grief in a triangle like that.

"Suppose I wanted to find Harley," I said. "Where should I look?"

"You'll see him tonight at the moonlight hayride. He'll be the guy driving the horses in the lead wagon."

"Hayride?" I blinked. "Horses?"

"Yeah, sure." Her hands stilled. "I'm surprised you don't already know about it. The hayride is a White Birch Inn tradition. Even when there's snow on the ground, Evelyn makes sure there's a clear path for it. The guys fill up a couple of wagons with hay, then all the guests pile in and ride around. The whole thing ends with a big bonfire at the foot of the mountain. Everyone's signed up for it unless they opt out."

I guessed that meant I was going on a hayride.

"You'll see." Catelyn winked at me. She was more relaxed now that we were no longer talking about Belinda. "The hayride's a great time. Everybody always loves it."

"Did you know there's a hayride tonight?" I asked when I got back to the room. Sam was already there. He and Faith were sitting on the love seat, and his laptop was open on the table in front of him.

"Sure. It was on our schedule." He closed his file, gazed up at me, and smiled. My heart did a little flip.

"Umm . . ."

"You did read the schedule, didn't you?"

"Not exactly." I sat down on Faith's other side and gave her a hug. "I knew you would, so I figured I was covered. Isn't it going to be freezing outside tonight?"

"Apparently in the low thirties, so I suppose it could be worse. According to the description, there will be plenty of hay, blankets, and spiked cider to keep us warm."

"With a bonfire at the end," I said.

"See? I knew you weren't entirely out of the loop." Sam stopped and sniffed the air. "I smell coconut."

"It's my hands." I held them out to him. "I had a hand massage."

"Okay." He looked bemused. "Why?"

"Because I wanted to talk to the masseuse and I needed a good excuse."

"This is about Belinda Rush, isn't it?" Sam knew me entirely too well.

"Yes," I admitted. "But before we get to that, how was the archery competition?"

"Fine. Chilly. Nonproductive from a win/lose point of view. Remind me never to enter an athletic event with your brother again. He couldn't hit a buffalo if it was standing right in front of him."

I laughed under my breath. Maybe I should have warned Sam about that ahead of time. Sports participation had never been Frank's strong suit.

"Why were you paired together?"

Sam frowned. "Because all the Valentine's activities are supposed to be for couples. So when we showed up together, we became a team."

I laughed again. Sam wasn't amused.

"Don't try to change the subject," he said. "Back to Belinda Rush."

"This time it wasn't my fault. Evelyn called me into her office and asked me to look into Belinda's death."

"Why?"

"Because the inn has been in her family for three generations and she's a businesswoman. She wants any questions about Belinda's death to be disposed of as quickly as possible."

Sam leaned back against the plump cushion. "I thought the sheriff was working on that."

"She is, but—"

His brow rose. "Evelyn just decided for no particular reason that you might be able to help out?"

"There was a reason," I said. "Bertie's a blabbermouth."

"I see." Sam's lips quirked.

"It's no big deal. We're only here for two more days, and I'm just going to ask some questions. I'm curious about what happened too."

"Why am I not surprised?" he asked.

I assumed that was a rhetorical question and felt free to ignore it.

"It's odd," I said instead. "So far I've only talked to a couple of people, but none of them seemed to know Belinda well. She was a young, vibrant woman, and nobody has much to say about her. That feels sad to me."

Sam nodded. "Sometimes people need to distance themselves from tragedy. It makes them feel safer. But it sounds to me as though Belinda needed someone to stand up for her. I'm happy that person is going to be you."

Chapter
Ten

The moonlight hayride was scheduled to start at eight p.m. By then, the sun had set and the air was crisp and cold. The sky above us was filled with stars.

Twenty couples showed up at the meeting place in front of the inn. Two wagons, their long, open beds filled to the brim with a cushion of straw, were waiting for us. With ten couples in each wagon, things were going to be cozy. Maybe that was the point.

Bertie and I were both wearing jeans, long underwear, and thick, woolen turtleneck sweaters. We had on boots, gloves, and scarves. Our parkas were zipped up to our chins. Sam and Frank were similarly bundled up. I hoped it was going to be enough to keep us warm.

Faith, who'd already had more than enough excitement for one day, had stayed behind in our room. She was probably relieved when we closed the door behind us and she was free to hop up on the bed and fall asleep.

Evelyn was supervising as members of the kitchen staff distributed thermoses of hot cider. While Sam, Bertie, and Frank got in line, I walked around to the front of the lead wagon. The two draft horses that would be pulling it were waiting patiently in their traces. Both were chestnut with flaxen manes and tails. Their lower legs were covered with thick feathering. Their hooves were the size of dinner plates.

I lifted a hand and touched a silky muzzle. The horse eyed me with interest. Maybe he was hoping I had a treat for him.

"That's Jess." A man walked around the side of the wagon. He was lean and wiry, and had a friendly smile. Reddish-brown hair peeked out from beneath his cowboy hat. He was wearing a flannel-lined denim jacket and heavyweight nubuck driving gloves. "He's big, but he's friendly. You can give him a pat if you want to. Joe here"—he nodded toward the other horse—"can get a little nippy sometimes, but Jess is a real people pleaser."

The description made me smile. "That sounds like a good kind of horse to have. Especially when they're this big."

"You got that right."

"You must be Harley," I said.

He tipped his head to one side and squinted at me.

Lights were on in front of the inn, but it was semi-dark on the driveway where we were standing. Still, I could see that the man's eyes were a steely shade of gray, and not nearly as friendly as his smile.

"Who wants to know?" he asked.

"I'm Melanie Travis. I'm staying at the inn for the weekend. Catelyn Hughes told me you'd be in charge tonight."

"In charge?" He shook his head. "No, I'll just be driving one of the wagons. You'd better go find your partner. It looks like it's time to load up."

I turned away and saw Sam heading toward me with a wool army blanket in one hand and a thermos in the other. "Frank and Bertie have climbed up into the next wagon," he told me. "I think Bertie's already burrowed down in the straw up to her neck. Let's go. They're saving us a spot."

"See you later," I said to Harley. He didn't reply, but I felt his gaze follow us as we walked to the rear of the second wagon.

"New friend?" Sam asked.

"The horse or the man?"

"Either one."

"I think the jury's still out on both of them."

Sam handed me up into the wagon, then followed behind. There was just enough room for us to wedge ourselves into the bed of straw beside Frank and Bertie. Though everyone squashed together pretty tightly, the mood in the wagon was jovial. People were already laughing and singing. I saw more than one person pull out a flask.

Our driver's name was Matt. He and Harley slapped their reins on the horses' backs in unison. The horses leaned into their harnesses and pulled. Slowly the wagons rolled down the long driveway. Bells were attached to the wagons' sides. They began to jingle cheerfully as soon as we were underway.

Sam unscrewed the cap off the thermos and handed it to me. "Be careful," he said as steam rose from inside the cylinder. "It looks hot."

"It is," Bertie confirmed. "I've already scalded my throat. But it was worth it. That cider has one heck of a kick. One more sip and I won't even remember it's freezing out here."

I took a small, cautious sip. Even so, the liquid burned all the way down my throat. It also cleared my sinuses. And there was a good chance that my hair was standing on end.

"Wow." I blinked several times. Suddenly even my toes were warm.

"That good?"

Sam was grinning. He took the thermos back from me, helped himself to a swallow, and came up coughing.

"I can see why they only allot one thermos per couple," he said when he'd gotten his breath back. "Any more than that, and we'd probably all be passed out by the time we got back to the inn."

"Not me," Bertie said happily. "I'm pacing myself. I intend to be fully cognizant when we reach the bonfire. I heard that one of these wagons is carrying twenty pounds of marshmallows for roasting over the fire."

For some reason, I found that enormously funny. "Twenty pounds? Marshmallows hardly weigh anything. How many would that be? Like a thousand?"

"I don't know and I don't care," Bertie replied. "As long as I get plenty of them."

The deep cushion of straw provided insulation from the cold. Sam and I spread the blanket across our laps and leaned back against the side of the wagon to gaze up at the stars. The rhythmic sway of the wagon and the measured beat of the horses' hooves striking the ground lulled me into a contented stupor.

Sam's hand found mine beneath the blanket. He'd taken off his glove. I did too. Our fingers intertwined and he squeezed gently.

"Happy Valentine's weekend," he murmured.

"Same to you," I replied.

Initially, I'd been skeptical about the pleasures of a nighttime hayride. But now, as I leaned over and rested my head on Sam's shoulder, I got it. All at once it was easy to understand why this was one of the inn's most popular events. If this wasn't a romantic experience, I couldn't imagine what would be.

Forty-five minutes later, the wagons drew up to a snow-covered clearing at the foot of the mountain. As far as I could tell, we had circled the surrounding neighborhoods twice and ended back up nearly where we'd started. Across the meadow, lights on the back of the inn reflected off the snow and the skating pond. It was a magical setting in which to end the evening.

We unloaded ourselves from the back of the wagon. The thermoses of cider had evidently done their job. Some people were more steady on their feet than others. Everyone was smiling however.

Matt led the two teams of horses several yards away and tethered them. Preparations for the bonfire had already been made in the middle of the clearing. Harley stepped forward and touched a fire starter to the tall stack of dried wood. Within seconds, there was a whoosh of sound as bright orange flames shot upward toward the sky.

Some people gasped. Others cheered in approval. I stood shoulder to shoulder with Sam and held on tight to his hand.

Bertie wasn't feeling as amorous as I was. Instead she was on the hunt for marshmallows. Within minutes she'd returned with a full bag and four metal skewers. "Choose your weapon," she said, holding them out to us.

Sam and Frank obliged her. I ripped open the plastic bag and popped an uncooked marshmallow in my mouth.

Bertie eyed me darkly. "That's sacrilege."

"Nope," I said, speaking around all that sugary goodness. "That's immediate gratification."

The toasted marshmallows were a huge hit. They became even better when graham crackers and chocolate squares were handed out too. More spiked cider was poured and drunk. Matt pulled out a guitar and began to play. Soon couples were singing and dancing around the fire.

After a while I noticed that Harley had removed himself from our noisy, exuberant gathering. He'd left the circle of golden light around the fire and was standing in the semidarkness near the teams of horses.

I touched Sam's arm lightly. "I'll be right back."

"Where are you going?"

"To see a man about a horse."

Sam watched as I skirted around the glowing embers at the base of the bonfire. Harley had his eyes on me too. Considering that I was one of the few partiers who was still capable of walking in a straight line, maybe I stood out. At least I hoped that was why he was looking at me.

Harley frowned as I approached. "Can I help you with something?"

"Do you mind if I ask you a couple of questions?"

He patted Jess's rump beside him. "About the horses?"

"No. About Belinda Rush."

"I don't know anything about her."

"That's not what I heard."

Harley crossed his arms over his chest and leaned back against the side of the wagon. He was the picture of nonchalance, except for his mouth, which was still drawn in a grim line. "You shouldn't believe everything you hear."

"So then you didn't know her?"

"That's not what I said. Of course I knew Belinda, or at least I knew who she was. There aren't that many of us who work and live here at the inn. Everybody gets acquainted on some level."

"But you were more than acquaintances, weren't you?"

Jess swished his flaxen tail. The tip of it caught Harley across the cheek. He swore under his breath, then straightened. Light from the bonfire played over his features as he leaned in close to me.

"Lady, I don't know where you're getting your information, but there was nothing between Belinda and me. It's a real shame what happened to her, the waste of a nice young woman. But as for my knowing anything about it, you're talking to the wrong person."

"If you're the wrong person, who should I ask?"

"Belinda had a guy in town," Harley replied. "I don't know who he was, and I don't care. I just know that for the last couple of weeks she was spending most of her free time away from the inn."

"Who would know more about him?" I asked.

Harley shrugged. He wasn't interested in continuing our conversation.

Back in the center of the clearing, the party was breaking up. People had stopped dancing in the firelight; now they were beginning to yawn. Matt was putting away his guitar.

"Excuse me." Harley shouldered his way past me. "I need to douse the fire. It's time to get everyone back to the inn."

I walked back to where Sam was waiting for me. He'd saved me one last s'more. I popped the sticky treat into my mouth and chewed blissfully.

"Learn anything interesting?" he asked.

Half a minute passed before I was able to answer. I took my time licking the last of the melted marshmallow off my lips. "No. Harley said that he and Belinda barely knew each other."

He peered at me in the flickering light. "It sounds as though you don't believe him."

"I don't. Harley was on the defensive before I even asked him a single question. Then he tried to send me on what's probably a fool's errand. I'm almost certain he was lying to me. And he wasn't even particularly good at it."

I sighed and stepped into the circle of Sam's arms. When I shivered slightly, he rubbed his hands up and down my back.

"You're cold."

"Not anymore." I snuggled closer.

"I need to get you back inside the inn."

"Soon," I murmured. "But let's have one last kiss in the moonlight first."

Chapter
Eleven

My phone rang early the next morning. It was on the night table beside the bed. I groaned and opened my eyes. Faith was sleeping on the love seat. She jumped up, came over, and nudged the phone with her nose. I grabbed it before it could fall to the floor."

Hi, Mom!" Kevin cried.

"Kev, is everything all right?"

I sat up. Faith took that as an invitation to hop up onto the bed. She settled down between Sam's legs and mine. The sun wasn't even up yet. I hoped I wasn't about to be dealing with an emergency of some kind.

"Everything's great," Kevin told me. "Aunt Peg lets us have pancakes for breakfast every morning. And we don't have to make our beds either."

That wasn't my definition of great, but okay. I could work with it.

"Why are you calling so early?" I asked.

"Because I'm awake," Kevin chortled. "And you answered the phone, so you're awake too."

"You can't fault that logic," said Sam.

He levered himself up against the headboard. The covers settled around his waist. He looked rumpled, and sleepy, and thoroughly sexy. Bad timing there. I put the phone on speaker and set it down on the pillow between us.

"Guess what?" asked Kevin.

"What?" I replied cautiously. For obvious reasons, this wasn't my favorite game.

"Aunt Peg got me a turtle. I named him Stanley."

Sam and I shared a look. In a house that was already full of dogs, we hardly needed another pet.

"Why?" I asked.

"Because he needed a home," Aunt Peg said crisply. She must have taken the phone from Kevin. "Some ghastly person was going to paint hearts and cupids on the turtles' shells and sell them for Valentine's Day. I bought out the entire lot before he had a chance to get busy with his paintbrush. Be glad you only ended up with one."

"What did you do with the rest of them?" Sam was biting back a grin.

"I gave them to the Nature Society. Along with a sizeable donation."

"Well done," I said. It was a relief to know she hadn't turned them loose in our backyard. "Other than that, how's everything going?"

"Splendidly." I was sure Aunt Peg wouldn't have it any other way. "How is your vacation shaping up?"

"Splendidly as well," I said.

"If you don't count the fact that Melanie has gotten herself mixed up in another mysterious—" Abruptly Sam stopped talking. He must have remembered that Kevin might be listening.

"Just a minute," Aunt Peg said, then her voice drifted away. "No, Kevin, you cannot put Stanley inside your backpack." A moment later, she was back. "I'm afraid you'll have to tell me about it another time—"

Abruptly the call disconnected. We hadn't even had a chance to say hello to Davey. I glanced over at Sam.

"Do you get the impression Aunt Peg is discovering that taking care of the boys might be more difficult than she'd anticipated?"

"Not just the boys," Sam said. "Her Poodles, our Poodles. And Bud. I'd imagine she has her hands full."

"Better her than us." I burrowed back down under the covers. "But if you'd like to have your hands full, I can think of a way we might spend the remaining hour until daylight."

*   *   *

When the sun finally rose over the mountain, it was another beautiful, clear day. After breakfast, Sam, Bertie, and Frank were going snowmobiling. I promised to join them later, but first I wanted to chat with Belinda's friend, Jill Lively. Hopefully Jill had had a closer relationship with Belinda than Catelyn did.

Head of hospitality for the inn, Jill Lively was a busy person, especially on an event-filled weekend when Belinda's death had left an unexpected void in the staff. I found her downstairs in the activities room, supervising its arrangement for the entertainment that afternoon.

Closer to thirty than twenty, Jill was petite and stick-thin. She was wearing a navy wool coatdress with brass buttons down the front, and she tottered around the room on a pair of four-inch spike heels that seemed particularly unsuited to our snowy surroundings. Then again, I'd just come back inside from walking Faith, which meant that I had on warm wool slacks and boots. Maybe she never left the inn during the day.

"Jill Lively?" I said from the doorway.

Inside the room, two men were setting up a series of long tables. A dolly carrying a row of folded metal chairs stood ready to be unpacked next. Jill was watching the men work, drumming her fingers impatiently on the top of a nearby cabinet.

She cast a quick glance my way, then paused and looked again. "Lovely Poodle. We haven't met, but that must be Faith?"

"She is," I confirmed. Faith liked hearing her name. She wagged her tail in acknowledgment. "I'm her owner, Melanie Travis. I didn't realize Faith was famous."

"Evelyn's the one who mentioned her. She's delighted that Sammy has a companion for the weekend. I'm afraid this room isn't open at the moment. We're setting up for this afternoon's bingo game."

"Bingo," I repeated.

Jill laughed at my obvious lack of enthusiasm. "Don't knock it until you've tried it. Our bingo isn't the geriatric game you're probably imagining. First, because we offer fantastic prizes. And second, because we lubricate the participants with unlimited alcohol, which makes our games surprising lively. You might want to grab your partner and stop by later. The event starts at two."

"I'll think about it," I said. Faith had left my side and was sniffing along the baseboard. Maybe Sammy had passed by recently. "In the meantime, do you have a few minutes to talk?"

"Sure, I guess so." Despite her words, Jill didn't look sure at all. "Go ahead."

There was a loud crash as one of the men started unloading the chairs. When he pulled the first one free, the next in line fell off the dolly and hit the linoleum floor. Faith jumped and hurried back to my side. This was not the right place for the conversation I wanted to have.

"Is there somewhere more private we could talk?" I asked Jill.

She looked surprised by the request, but recovered quickly. "My office is right around the corner. If you want, we can go there."

In contrast to Evelyn's cozy office upstairs, Jill's basement space was chilly and stark. Not only was there no rug or fireplace, she didn't even have a window. Jill had attempted to brighten the plain white walls by hanging up several colorful travel posters, all featuring sunny tropical locales. They didn't help much.

Her desk was made of metal and wood laminate. The single visitor chair matched those I'd just seen in the activities room. Clearly Jill didn't get many drop-in guests. There was a space heater in the corner. She walked over and turned it on. Then she closed the door and we both sat down.

Faith declined to lie down on the cold floor. Instead she sat on her haunches and placed her head in my lap. *Good.* That would provide both of us with a little warmth.

"I know," Jill muttered, although I hadn't said a

thing. "Some hospitality, right? But around here the money gets spent where guests are going to see it."

She stopped abruptly and covered her mouth with her hands. "Sorry! I shouldn't have said that. I'm just having a bad day."

"I understand."

Jill opened a drawer in her desk and pulled out a pen and a pad of paper. "Please tell me what I can do to help you. The White Birch Inn strives to offer the highest level of service. I hope you haven't come to lodge a complaint, but if so, I assure you I will do everything in my power to make things right."

I was smiling when she finished. "You sound like you memorized the personnel handbook."

"Just about. Thankfully, I don't have to make that speech often." She leaned forward and folded her hands together on top of the desk. "Seriously, what can I do for you?"

"I'd like to talk to you about Belinda Rush."

Immediately Jill's face clouded over. She exhaled a shuddering sigh.

"You and Belinda were friends," I said.

"Yes."

"I'm sorry."

"Thank you. Belinda didn't deserve that." Jill swallowed heavily. "Whatever *that* is. Evelyn told us the police think she died of exposure."

"So I heard."

"Well, it doesn't make sense to me. Belinda was from upstate New York. She knew all about cold weather. And why was she even out there in the middle of the night, anyway?"

"I don't know," I admitted. "I was hoping you might have some ideas."

She stared at me across the desktop. "What does this have to do with you?"

"Evelyn asked me to see what I could find out."

Jill looked incredulous. *"Evelyn asked you . . . ?"* Then her eyes widened. "Oh wait. I get it. Evelyn's afraid that Belinda's death could be bad for business. Right?"

"Something like that."

"That's ridiculous," she snapped. "To be worrying about the *business* as if that's all that matters."

Jill shoved back her chair and stood up. She began to pace around the small room. "I'll tell you what *matters*. Belinda Rush was a good person. Maybe because she was quiet, not everyone had a chance to see that. But Bel was the kind of person who always wanted to help. If someone had a problem, she'd be first in line to listen—and to see what she could do to make things better."

"How long had you known her?" I asked.

"Since she came to work here six months ago." Jill thought back. "She was excited about getting the job.

And about living at the inn. We both have rooms in the dorm upstairs."

I nodded. I already knew that. "A minute ago, you said that you couldn't understand how Belinda died. Can you think of any reason why someone might have wanted to harm her?"

"Harm her?" Jill walked over to the desk and sat back down. "Like maybe her death wasn't an accident?"

"It's a possibility," I said. "Had anything changed recently in Belinda's life? Her behavior? Her friends? The way she did her job?"

Jill frowned, then nodded slowly. "Actually there was something I wondered about."

Faith whined under her breath and pressed her rib cage against my legs. She was probably chilly. I reached down and pulled the front half of her body up into my lap.

"What was that?"

"Weekdays, Evelyn likes to keep the inn's schedule filled with single-day special events. We host corporate retreats, conferences, various club outings, and even team-building exercises. Which means we often have a lot of people coming in and out in a short period of time."

"That makes sense," I said.

"Belinda and I worked together on all those things. She was great under that kind of pressure, probably the most organized person I'd ever met. She made lists of everything and nothing ever seemed to faze her."

"She sounds like a good partner," I said. "I can see why you would have enjoyed working with her."

"Believe me, having Belinda here made my job *much* easier," Jill replied. "But recently the way she handled her duties began to change. It seemed to me that Belinda was singling out some of the attendees for special attention. She'd even go so far as to follow them around. I'd imagine she was just making sure they had everything they needed, but still . . ."

"Is that unusual?" I asked. "Don't the more important clients always receive extra attention?"

"Yes, of course. But as far as I could tell there was nothing about these guests that set them apart. They weren't our corporate liaisons, or the people who'd booked the site. And if Evelyn had requested preferential treatment for them, I'm sure she'd have told me too, since Belinda's and my jobs worked hand in hand."

"That does seem odd," I mused. I had no idea what to make of it. "Did you ask Belinda about it?"

"I did. She just laughed and told me I was imagining things. She said there was no way she would play favorites among the hotel guests."

Jill stood up again. It was time for her to get back to work. I nudged Faith back down to the floor, then stood up too.

"One last question," I said. "Did Belinda have a boyfriend?"

"I don't know." Jill frowned.

"That's surprising. It sounds to me as though you and she talked about a lot of things."

"We did. But not that, at least not in specifics. If I had to guess, I'd say there might have been someone because there were times it felt like she was purposely keeping mum about something. But Bel never volunteered who the guy was, so I respected her privacy."

Jill started toward the door. Faith and I followed.

"I heard that Belinda might have been seeing someone in town," I said. "She never mentioned a name to you?"

"Someone in town?" Jill was surprised. "I had no idea. Do you think that's important? Like maybe he had something to do with what happened?"

"I don't know," I told her. "But I'd like to find out."

"Hmm . . ." She paused to consider. "I might be able to help with that."

Faith had already beaten both of us to the door. But Jill had stopped walking. Now I did too. Like we both suspected that maybe this wasn't a conversation we wanted to have out in the corridor.

"How?" I asked.

"Belinda's room upstairs is right next to mine," Jill said. "And I know where she kept her spare key."

Chapter
Twelve

Okay, confession time. I always wanted to be Nancy Drew when I grew up. And now—with Jill offering the prospect of a spare key to Belinda's room—it felt like this might be about as close to emulating that sleuth as I'd ever get. I couldn't wait to say yes.

Jill went to get the key and I ran Faith upstairs to our room. She'd be much safer there. It was one thing for Jill and I to conduct a clandestine mission inside the inn, but Faith always drew attention. She was hard to miss.

I'd agreed to meet Jill on the third-floor landing in five minutes. I was closing the door to my room, about to speed upstairs, when Bertie emerged from her room next door.

I stopped, surprised. "What are you doing here? I thought you were out snowmobiling with the guys."

"I was. But it turned out that mostly what they wanted to do was drive too fast, slide on the icy snow, and skid around sharp corners. After ten minutes, I'd had enough of that."

"Men," I said.

She nodded. "So I came back here to see what you were up to. I was just dropping off my outdoor gear, then I was going to come looking for you."

While inside my room, I'd exchanged my boots for running shoes. Bertie was wearing the same. Perfect. We were both dressed for sneaking around.

Maybe I was getting a little too into my Nancy Drew vibe.

"I'm going on a mission," I said, grabbing her arm. "And now that you're here, you're coming too."

"What kind of mission?" Bertie was ever practical. She wanted specifics before she committed.

There was no one else in the hallway. I lowered my voice anyway. "We're going to search Belinda's room."

"What?" Bertie pulled back. "You're kidding, right?"

"Nope. Dead serious." I began to tug her in the direction of the stairway. "Don't flake on me now. We've got work to do."

"You are such a bad influence," she muttered, following reluctantly. "If we get arrested, you're paying my bail."

"We're not going to get arrested," I told her. "You can be George to my Nancy."

Bertie, bless her, understood the reference right away. "Honestly, I've always felt like more of a Bess."

"Bess is the timid one. She's afraid of adventure. That's definitely not you," I said. "Now hurry up. I'll explain on the way."

Jill was already waiting by the time we reached the third-floor landing. She stared at Bertie suspiciously. "Who are you?"

"George," said Bertie. She extended her hand. Neither woman looked particularly pleased to meet the other.

"She's my best friend," I said. "Don't worry, she knows how to keep her mouth shut." Suddenly, for some reason I was talking like I was in a 1940s gangster movie.

Jill still didn't look happy, but she led the way to a plain door at the end of the hall. A sign on it said STAFF ONLY.

"This stairway leads to the staff quarters in the attic," she told us. "It's pretty basic up there, but since this is a resort area, most of the employees can't afford to live in town. So we're lucky to have rooms we can call our own. Belinda's room is second to last on the right."

Jill held out her hand. A small key was resting in her palm.

"Wait," I said. "You're not coming with us?"

"Not a chance." She was already backing away. "If you get caught, you can probably talk your way out of it. Just say you got lost or something. If I get caught, I'll lose my job. I'm not risking that."

"Bess," Bertie muttered under her breath.

I covered a sudden laugh with a cough.

Jill stared at the two of us like we were nuts. "Be sure to bring that back to me as soon as you're finished," she said, nodding toward the key. "I want to return it before it has a chance to be missed."

"Will do," I told her.

Bertie and I waited until Jill was gone before opening the door. A draft of cool air greeted us. The enclosed stairway leading up to the attic was narrow compared to the sumptuous staircase meant for guests, but it was carpeted and well lit.

"After you, Nancy," Bertie said.

"You know that's going to get old pretty quickly."

"Maybe." She closed the door behind us. "But I intend to get full use out of it until it does."

When I reached the top of the steps, I could see all the way down the long attic corridor. Thankfully, it was empty. Midmorning, most of the dorm's inhabitants should have been busy at their jobs. Even so, I had no intention of pressing my luck. My plan was to be in and out of Belinda's room in under ten minutes.

Bertie and I crept down the hallway. Which was

probably silly since there was no one around to see or hear us. When we reached the room we'd been told was Belinda's, I quickly unlocked the door with the key. Bertie and I slipped inside.

The room was bigger and more comfortable than I'd expected. A single bed, covered with a flower-print duvet, was pushed up against one wall. A vertical chest of drawers sat opposite it. There was a small closet just inside the door, and a compact desk beneath the window. Icicles hung from the eaves just outside, but it was warm enough in here.

Belinda had hung a cork bulletin board and a calendar featuring pictures of kittens on the wall. Her bed was neatly made. A hardcover book—Harlan Coben's latest thriller—was splayed open on the pillow, possibly to mark the page she'd been reading when she left.

The closet held several changes of clothing and four pairs of shoes. A toiletries kit and a fluffy bath towel were hanging from a rack on the back of the door. Bertie and I had passed the communal bathroom on our way down the hall.

Two framed photographs were displayed on top of the dresser. Both looked like they'd been taken on vacation. In one, Belinda was standing in front of the Eiffel Tower, pointing up at the landmark with a big smile on her face. In the other, she and a man were sitting on a beach. The two of them had their arms around each other's shoulders.

Even though I'd only known Belinda briefly, seeing these pictures of her in happier times made my breath lodge in my throat.

"Is it just me," Bertie whispered, "or does this feel kind of creepy to you? Like we're invading Belinda's privacy."

"I wish she was still here to care." I sighed. I hadn't expected that seeing Belinda's room—filled with her belongings as though she was about to return at any moment—would hit me so hard. "Let's just get this over with, okay?"

The opportunity to look through Belinda's things had been fortuitous. So I hadn't had time to make a plan. Now I had no idea what I was looking for, or what I might expect to find. A diary would have been helpful. Or maybe an address book with a list of important contacts. I got out my phone and snapped a picture of both photographs.

Bertie rifled through Belinda's desk. There were only two small drawers. One held a couple of pens and pencils, along several Sudoku puzzle books. The other had a box of stationery, a pair of scissors, paper clips, and a roll of tape. Hardly scintillating stuff.

Bertie looked behind the bulletin board, then thumbed through the pages of the hanging calendar.

All were unmarked. She reached across the desk and shook out the curtains.

I opened Belinda's dresser drawers and looked under her bed. I checked the pockets of her clothing and looked inside her shoes. I even lifted the edges of the rug and peered beneath them.

Time was passing quickly. It was beginning to look as though I'd dragged Bertie along on a wild goose chase.

"You know what our problem is?" She stood in the center of the room and gazed around. "Someone's beaten us to it. Where are Belinda's laptop and her purse? What happened to her phone? That's where we'd have been most likely to find something interesting."

"The police probably have those things," I said. "Don't you think?"

Bertie frowned. "Either that, or the person who left her outside in the snow to die came here afterward and took them."

"They would have needed her key," I pointed out.

"Right. And how hard was that for *us* to come by?"

She and I shared a nervous look as the reality of our situation suddenly hit home.

"I guess we'd better get out of here before someone comes upstairs," I said. "I'd really rather not have to explain why we engaged in this exercise in futility."

I reached the door and turned around. Bertie was staring at the novel on Belinda's bed.

"What?"

"Belinda was a mystery fan."

I had no idea why that mattered. "Good for her?"

Bertie was already walking over to the bed. "I read this in a book once. A guy hid something he didn't want anyone to find inside his pillow."

She reached for Belinda's pillow and lifted it up. The thriller that had been on top of it slid off to one side. Bertie peered into the pillowcase. Then she stuck her hand inside.

"What's in there?" Eagerly I stepped closer.

"Nothing so far. I'm just fishing around."

"Try taking the case off," I suggested.

"That was my next plan." Bertie tossed the empty pillowcase back on the bed. The pillow appeared to be stuffed with feathers. It was sewn shut.

I felt my way along the edges. Then I pushed down in the middle. I didn't feel anything.

"There are scissors in the desk," Bertie said.

I considered only briefly before shaking my head. "We can't cut the pillow open. If we do, it'll be obvious that someone searched Belinda's room."

Bertie made a gagging noise. Abruptly I realized that the same dismaying thought had just occurred to both of us. We weren't wearing gloves.

"Okay," I said briskly. " Now it's really time to go. Let's put everything back exactly the way it was and get the heck out of here."

Bertie stuffed the pillow back into its case and tossed it toward the head of the bed. I reached over and grabbed the book. Its colorful jacket had come unhooked from the back cover when it tumbled off the pillow. With clumsy, hurrying fingers, I turned the book around and tried to slip the jacket back where it belonged.

For a moment, the slick paper resisted my attempts to make its crease slip into place. "Damn it," I swore under my breath. Then all at once I realized something. My fingers stopped moving.

The book jacket should have felt nearly weightless in my hands. It didn't.

Bertie was already standing by the door. "Hurry *up*," she said. "If you can't get it on right, just leave it. Nobody will notice."

Suddenly I wasn't so sure about that.

I opened the book's front cover and slipped the jacket off entirely. My breath caught. A slender piece of paper was taped to its inside. A list of numbers was written on it in pencil.

I glanced over at Bertie. She quickly crossed the small room.

"What is that?"

"Numbers," I said. "Some kind of list."

I loosened the tape with my fingers and gently peeled the paper free. Bertie grabbed the book jacket, slid it back on, and spread the book open across the pillow. I folded the small piece of paper and slipped it in my pocket. Then we both hurried back to the door.

"What do you think it means?" she asked.

"It means that Belinda had something to hide. Maybe something important enough to get her killed."

Chapter
Thirteen

Bertie went straight back to our rooms. I ran the key downstairs to Jill's office.

She glanced up as I entered. "Did you find anything?"

I shrugged and laid the key to Belinda's room on her desk. I wasn't about to mention the piece of paper that suddenly felt as though it was burning a hole in my pocket. Not until I knew what it meant and whom it might implicate.

"Just this." I showed her the picture on my phone. "Do you know who the guy is? He and Belinda look pretty cozy."

Jill leaned forward and peered at the picture. "I've never seen him before. But I also don't think that's a recent picture. Look how much longer Bel's hair is. Now she wore it just below her chin. There, it's all the way down to her shoulders."

Darn it. I should have noticed that myself. Maybe I would have if I hadn't been in such a hurry.

Jill settled back in her chair. "So if Belinda had a boyfriend in town, I don't think that's the guy."

"Too bad." I put my phone away. "I was hoping it might be a clue."

Her lips quirked. "You wanted to be Nancy Drew and ride to the rescue, didn't you?"

"Something like that," I admitted. It sounded stupid when Jill said it out loud.

"What's your friend's real name? I'm sure it isn't George."

"Bertie."

"Birdy, like with wings?"

That would have made Bertie laugh. "No, Bertie, like Alberta."

"Well, you can tell her she wasn't far off when she called me Bess. I do like to stay safe. Looking before I leap has always served me well in the past."

"Then thank you even more for your help," I said. "I know you took a risk just getting me the key."

Jill waved away my thanks. "Belinda was a good person. She's the one I wanted to help. If someone did that to her intentionally, I'd like to see that person fry in hell."

* * *

Upstairs, I found Bertie sitting on the love seat in Sam's and my room, playing with Faith.

"What are you doing here?" I asked. "I thought you'd be next door."

"Faith let me in." Her expression was deadpan.

"Faith is smart, but not that smart," I said. "Besides she can't open the door. She doesn't have opposable thumbs."

"Sam gave Frank a spare key to your room," she told me.

"He did? Why?"

"In case of emergency." Bertie frowned my way. "Don't give me that look. You know perfectly well what I mean. When you're around, sometimes things go south in a hurry. So Sam gave us access, just in case. That's all it was. Don't overthink it."

It was hard not to. Did Sam think that living with me was actually that much of a risk? Thankfully, before I had a chance to answer that question, Bertie changed the subject.

"Come on, gimme. Let's have a look at that paper."

I slid it carefully out of my pocket and handed it over. Bertie unfolded the small sheet and laid it on the low table in front of the love seat. Then she scooted over to make room for me.

As soon as I sat down, Faith snuggled her body

against mine. She lifted her long muzzle and licked the underside of my chin. It hadn't even been an hour since she and I were together, but Faith was letting me know that it was entirely too long.

"I know," I crooned. "I missed you too."

I rested one hand on her back and burrowed my fingers into her warm coat. My other hand rubbed her favorite spot just beneath her ear. Faith sighed happily. Once again, all was right with her world.

Bertie was staring at the paper intently. "What do you make of it?"

The penciled writing was faint and difficult to read. I leaned in closer. There were six short sets of numbers. Each number was followed by a single letter.

1230 c
110 h
121 j
130 h
211 c

"This is like those number puzzles in math that I was never very good at," I grumbled. "We're supposed to figure out something they all have in common, right? Or look for a progression of some kind?"

"They all start with one except the last number," Bertie mused. "Maybe that means something."

"And they all end with either one or zero," I pointed out.

We both sat and stared for another minute.

"If you look at the first two digits of each number, you have 12, 11, 12, 13, 21," Bertie said. "The last one, 21, seems out of place in that group."

"Right. And the first number is the only one with four digits. That's also different than the others. And two of the letters are repeated, and one isn't. What do you suppose that means?"

Bertie shrugged. She was as baffled as I was. We sat and thought some more. Which would have been a great strategy if time alone was going to solve the puzzle. Faith hopped down and went to get a drink of water. Apparently we were boring her.

It looked as though my important clue was turning out to be a bust.

"Wait!" Bertie cried suddenly. "I think I have something. If I'm right, those numbers *are* in sequence. Because they're dates."

"Dates?" I looked again and realized she could be right.

She read them aloud one by one. "December 30, January 10, January 21, January 30, February 11."

"Five dates, all approximately ten days apart. Bertie, you're a genius."

"I know." She preened. "Lucky for you."

"You're right because I wasn't even close to coming up with that."

Then I checked the list again and my stomach dropped. Suddenly my buoyant mood vanished. "Belinda must have added the last date on Thursday, the day we arrived at the inn."

"And the day she died," Bertie said.

Sam and Frank got back just in time for lunch. Sam's nose and cheeks were sunburned, which made his eyes look even more blue than usual. When he took off his cap, his blond hair stood straight up. Both guys were grinning happily and congratulating each other on their exploits. At least they'd managed to make it back in one piece.

"You missed a great time," Frank said to Bertie. "I can't believe you wanted to bail out early."

"Frank nearly hit a tree," Sam told us.

"It was this close." Frank held up two fingers barely three inches apart. Incredibly, he sounded proud of himself. "I ended up with twigs in my hair."

As if that was something to brag about.

I pulled a tube of sunscreen out of my open suitcase and walked over to Sam. "Next time, don't forget this."

He glanced over at the mirror and did a double take when he saw his image. Sam took the tube from me, squeezed out a generous dollop of sunscreen, and applied it to his face.

"That's for when you're outside," I said with a laugh. "Not in here."

"It turns out that lunch is an outdoor picnic," he said. "Frank and I heard about it on the way in. They were setting up tables over by the skating pond."

"Hearty beef stew, roasted asparagus, sourdough bread, and hot toddies." Frank licked his lips. "Yum!"

When we walked outside behind the inn half an hour later, more than a dozen couples were already assembled around a fire pit where a huge pot of beef stew was simmering. Even from a distance, it smelled wonderful.

Faith, who was beside me, suddenly lifted her head and wagged her tail. I looked to see what had caught her eye. Sammy was racing around the other side of the snow-covered meadow. It looked as though he had a loaf of sourdough bread in his mouth.

"Go ahead," I told her. "Just don't go too far away."

Faith was off like a shot. The white Samoyed and the big black Poodle made a striking pair. More than one person turned to admire the two dogs as they frolicked through the low drifts.

There was a short line to pick up food. Sam, Bertie,

and Frank headed that way. I had another idea. Molly and Trina had already been served. They were sitting together at one of the picnic tables.

"I'll be right back," I said to Sam. "Save me a place in line."

Molly smiled as I slid onto the bench across from them. Trina had a mouthful of stew. She gave me a little wave.

Both women were both bundled up against the chilly weather. Molly looked warm and comfy in a fuchsia faux fur that should have clashed with her red hair but somehow didn't. Trina was dressed entirely in white from head to toe. Like Sammy, she matched the snowy backdrop.

"You're the Poodle lady," Molly said.

In my life, that's usually Aunt Peg's title. But I didn't mind standing in for her in her absence.

"That's me," I said. "How are you two doing?"

Trina swallowed, then said, "Better, I guess. Although it's still a shock, what happened. Molly and I definitely won't be coming back here again."

I nodded. I could understand that. "Before she died, Belinda wrote down a list of dates. I wonder if they mean anything to you?"

Before we came down to lunch I'd copied the list over, separating and punctuating the numbers so they made more sense. Then I'd left the original in a safe place. I passed my copy to them across the table. Both women scanned it briefly.

"It doesn't mean a thing to me." Molly bit off a hunk of bread.

"Me either," Trina agreed. She passed the paper back.

It was a long shot, but I'd figured it was worth checking.

"There's something else I was wondering about," I said. "You said that Belinda invited the two of you here for the weekend. Had she ever done that before?"

Molly and Trina looked at each other. They both shook their heads.

"Then why now?"

"Maybe Valentine's Day made her think of us," Molly guessed. The thought made her smile, and I belatedly realized that the two of them were a couple.

"I wondered about that too," Trina said. "I wondered if it meant that Belinda was getting itchy feet again. Like maybe she was bored with stability and getting ready to move on."

"Or maybe she just needed a couple of warm bodies." Molly shrugged. "Don't forget, Belinda had all these rooms to fill. We were probably easy to book compared to all the vendors Evelyn made her jampack the ballroom with."

I straightened in my seat as Faith and Sammy zoomed across my line of vision. The two dogs were still keeping each other entertained. "Belinda told you that was Evelyn's idea?"

"Sure," Trina replied. "She wanted us to know ahead of time that there'd be plenty of shopping opportunities. Plus, now that we're here, the vendors have been bitching about it."

They must have heard the same kinds of complaints that Bertie and I had. "You mean the overcrowding? And the competition to attract shoppers?"

"It's more than that," Molly said. "Trina and I have spent so much time in the ballroom most of the vendors know us by name. They tell us things that they probably wouldn't say to just anybody."

"Like what?"

Trina lowered her voice. "Belinda double-booked vendors who were selling the most popular items. When they arrived and saw the situation wasn't what they'd been promised, some of them complained to Belinda. She sent them to Evelyn."

Molly picked up the story. "Evelyn then pitted the vendors against each other—offering longer selling hours and preferred positions to those who'd give her a bigger cut of their business than they'd previously agreed upon."

"That's extortion," I said.

Trina nodded. "Evelyn said anyone who objected

to the higher rates could pack up and go home. Since they'd already come all the way out here, most of them decided to make the best of it. Even if they weren't happy with the arrangements."

"Why would Evelyn do something like that?" I asked.

"For the money." Molly smirked. "Why else?"

"Because she could," Trina added. "And because there wasn't a thing they could do to stop her."

Faith and Sammy were still playing in the snow when I sat down next to Sam, and across from Bertie and Frank.

"Your stew is getting cold," Sam said. He'd filled a plate for me when the three of them had reached the front of the line and gotten their food.

"And I stole your bread," Frank mentioned, chewing happily. His own plate looked like it had been licked clean. "Because it's not like you were here to eat it."

"That was rude." I dug into my beef stew. Even barely warm, it was delicious.

"Here." Sam passed a steaming mug my way. "Have a hot toddy. They mixed them strong. It will make you forget all about your lost bread."

"Bread?" Bertie gave me a goofy grin. "It will make you forget your children's names."

"How many of those have you had?" I asked.

Bertie held up one finger. A moment later, a second one joined it. She looked at her hand in surprise as if that was news to her, and didn't seem to notice when the rest of us laughed.

"I think I'll stick to eating my stew," I decided.

"Good idea," said Sam.

Chapter
Fourteen

After lunch, it was time for couples' ice skating. That was so *not* me. Nor Sam either, apparently. He didn't look any more enthused about the idea than I was.

"Several dozen pairs of novice skaters trying to look romantic while they wobble around the ice and crash into each other? No thank you. I'm not looking to break any bones this afternoon." Sam paused and looked at me. "That is, unless you want to do it?"

"Not me," I said. "I'm out."

Faith came trotting over to the picnic table. There were snowballs in her ear feathers and tail pompon. Her mouth was open, her tongue sliding in and out. She looked tired, but very happy. I beckoned and she came to my side.

"I'm game," Bertie announced. "And for the record, I'm a perfectly good skater."

I peered at her. Her eyes appeared to be slightly unfocused. "Are you sure that's not just the hot toddies talking?"

She straightened in surprise. "They can talk?"

Frank laughed and slipped an arm around her shoulder. "I think we'd better save the skating for later. I'm taking you back to the room."

Bertie's eyebrows waggled. "You just want to have your wicked way with me."

"Yes, dear."

"Okay." Bertie rose to her feet, somewhat unsteadily. "Just as long as we understand each other."

"I'll tell you what I don't understand," I said to Sam as the two of them walked away. "What does Bertie see in him?"

Sam chuckled under his breath.

"Truly. She has a lot of great things going for her. She could do better."

"Love works in mysterious ways."

That was no kind of explanation at all. He probably couldn't figure it out either.

Sam reached over and stroked Faith's muzzle.

"Since we're not going skating, what do you want to do this afternoon?"

"Actually, I'd like to take a trip into town."

"Oh? Any place in particular you want to go?"

"The sheriff's office."

Sam didn't look entirely surprised. "You've already talked to Sheriff Finley once."

"Yes, but that was right after Evelyn told everyone that Belinda Rush's death was an accident. At that point, the sheriff was still waiting to see what the medical examiner's report would reveal. Now I'm hoping she has new information."

Sam nodded. "Then I suppose we should head into town."

Steepleton was a quaint New England town whose four main streets formed a square around the village green. Well-shoveled walking paths, currently empty, led to a gabled roof gazebo in the center of the space. At a time when big box merchandising had put so many local shops out of business, commerce appeared to be thriving in Steepleton. Stores were not only open, but their windows had been decorated for the holiday. Many were covered with festive images of hearts and flowers.

In contrast, the sheriff's office was all business. It was a plain, brick, one-story building, located next door to the town hall. There was an open parking place not too far away and Sam slipped his SUV into it.

On the way to town, I'd told him everything I'd learned so far about Belinda's life. Sam often makes a good sounding board, but this time he didn't have much to add. That probably wasn't his fault. My thoughts about Belinda's death were so jumbled that I was having a hard time making sense of them too.

"I'll take Faith for a stroll while you talk to the sheriff," Sam said. "How long do you think you'll be?"

"I guess that depends on how eager she is to see me." My previous experiences with law enforcement hadn't been entirely positive, and my first conversation with Sheriff Finley had done little to make me think that was about to change.

"Call me when you're done then. We'll be around town somewhere."

I nodded and went inside.

Sheriff Finley was seated behind her desk when I was shown into her office. She didn't rise. Nor did she appear particularly curious about why I was there. Even sitting down, the woman possessed an authoritative presence that dominated the room. All at once I felt more like a supplicant than someone who might have useful information to share.

The office was spacious with windows that offered a wide view of the green and the downtown area. Framed commendations filled the walls. Sheriff Finley had been reading through a packet of papers when I entered. Grudgingly, she set them aside. There was a half-full coffee mug on her desk with a pink lipstick stain around the rim. Its slogan read *TOP COP*.

There was a single chair on the visitor side of the desk. I took it without requesting permission. The sheriff raised a brow. I pretended not to notice.

It was cold inside the room. Maybe Sheriff Finley wanted everyone who entered to be reminded of how tough she was. I wasn't tough at all—but for the few minutes I was going to be there, I could do a good job of pretending. I unzipped my parka, took it off, and draped it across my lap.

The sheriff watched all this without comment. She hadn't said a single thing since I'd walked through her doorway.

"I'm Melanie Travis," I said. "We met yesterday at the White Birch Inn."

"I remember."

"I might have some information for you."

"Go on."

I wondered if every answer she gave me would consist of just two words.

"I don't think Belinda Rush's death was an accident."

Sheriff Finley's eyes narrowed slightly. It was the first reaction I'd managed to elicit from her. It earned me two more words.

"Why not?"

"The man I told you about yesterday—the one I saw with Belinda the night she died—is Cliff Granger, the inn's lifeguard."

Finley nodded. Apparently that wasn't news.

"Did he confirm what I told you?" I asked.

"He did. He also told me that when he and Belinda

parted ways, just a few minutes after you saw them, Belinda was fine."

Finally, a full sentence—even if it was one that didn't sound particularly credible to me. "And you believed him?"

Finley looked annoyed. Apparently I wasn't supposed to be the one asking questions. "Let's just say that at the moment, I don't have a reason not to believe him."

"He threatened me," I said. "Maybe he threatened Belinda too. Maybe he went even further and acted upon his threats."

"How did Mr. Granger threaten you?" Finally, I'd managed to pique her curiosity.

"He approached me at the inn and told me to stay out of his business or I'd be sorry."

"So," she said calmly. "Not a threat of specific harm."

"It felt specific enough to me," I muttered.

"Your discomfort is noted."

As if that should make me feel better.

This line of conversation was getting me nowhere. I tried another approach. "I heard that Belinda had been pressured into overbooking the vendors who've come to the inn for the holiday weekend. Apparently, many of them are angry about that."

Sheriff Finley had started to reach for a pen. Abruptly she paused. "Pressured by whom?"

"The inn's owner."

Evelyn and the sheriff had seemed pretty friendly with each other the previous day. Since they both held influential positions in the small town, it made sense that their relationship would be cordial and cooperative. That thought was enough to make me reassess what I'd been about to say. With the sheriff staring at me skeptically, it didn't seem entirely prudent to divulge *all* the details Molly and Trina had shared with me.

"Surely you don't think a little overcrowding could have led to Ms. Rush's death?" she asked.

"No, but the way the vendors were treated did make me wonder whether the inn might be having financial problems. Do you know if that's the case?"

"I do not." The pen was in Finley's hand now. She tapped it on the desk in an agitated beat. "And if I did know, I wouldn't tell you. You are merely a short-term guest in my community, Ms. Travis. There's no need for you to be privy to my neighbors' secrets."

What if one of your neighbors' secrets got Belinda killed? I wondered. The possibility that I might be right about that was the only reason I didn't stand up and walk out.

"I have something to show you," I said. "Two things, actually."

I reached over and placed the paper Bertie and I had found in Belinda's room on her desk. I put the reconfigured copy next to it. Sheriff Finley glanced at both papers, then lifted her gaze.

"What am I looking at?"

"The list on your left was written by Belinda. The second list is a copy I made with the numbers rewritten as dates."

The sheriff took another look. "Is this supposed to mean something to me?"

"I hope so," I replied. "Those dates must have meant something to Belinda. I'm sure the list was important to her. Otherwise she wouldn't have bothered to hide it."

That brought Finley's attention back to me in a hurry. "How exactly did you happen to come across this secret list?"

I'd known the question would be coming. I'd decided ahead of time that this was one of those sticky situations where honesty was going to have to be the best policy. Whether I liked it or not.

"I found it in Belinda's room," I said.

"Her room," she repeated incredulously. "You mean her room at the inn?"

"Yes."

The sheriff's voice took on a dangerous edge. "When was this, and what made you think that her room was a place you ought to be?"

"I found the list earlier today," I said. "And I was

there because Evelyn asked me to look into Belinda's death."

Okay, that wasn't strictly true. Evelyn had told me to observe and ask questions, not to break into a locked room. But Sheriff Finley wouldn't know that. At least not until she had a chance to compare notes with Evelyn. And hopefully by then, I would be long gone.

"*Evelyn* did?"

"Yes." It was hard not to flinch with the sheriff's steely gaze trained my way.

"I find that hard to believe."

"Ask her yourself." I shrugged with a nonchalance I was far from feeling. "Death is bad for business. Evelyn wants to know why Belinda died so she can move on and put the whole tragic episode behind her."

To my surprise, Sheriff Finley suddenly looked tired. "That won't be happening," she said. "The report from the postmortem was on my desk when I came back from lunch. Ms. Rush didn't freeze to death as we initially thought. A toxic concentration of oxycodone was found in her blood and urine."

I gasped softly. "Belinda overdosed on opioids?"

"I'm afraid so."

More questions immediately came to mind. "Was it an accident? Or could someone have done that to her?"

"We have no way of knowing at the moment," Finley replied. "But obviously that knowledge changes the scope of our investigation."

The sheriff gazed toward her window and the village green that lay beyond it. "It's tempting to believe that our small mountain town is a haven of decency and morality. But unfortunately we're no more immune to the ills that infect society than anywhere else. Drugs are one of the leading causes of death in this country no matter where you live."

"I'm aware of that," I said.

She blinked, then stared at me. For a moment, I think she'd almost forgotten I was there. "You said this paper came from Ms. Rush's room. Now I want you to think very carefully before you answer—did you remove anything else when you were there?"

"No, of course not."

Finley gave me the look that comment probably deserved.

"I didn't," I said. "But Belinda's phone, laptop, and purse were all missing from her room. I thought maybe your office had taken them."

"We did not," Sheriff Finley replied. "There didn't appear to be a need. Until I saw this report, I thought we were dealing with a different problem entirely."

She looked down at the two papers I'd left on her desk. This time, she took a minute to study them. "I can see why you thought the numbers might refer to dates. Do you know what the letters after them mean?"

"Unfortunately, no."

"February eleventh," she mused. "That was just two days ago."

"It was also the day Belinda was last seen alive."

Finley looked up sharply. "Surely she wasn't referencing her own death."

"Let's hope not." I stood up and put on my jacket. Our talk hadn't been entirely successful, but it had given both of us some new things to think about.

"I'm keeping these," she said, gathering up the papers I'd brought with me.

"I figured you would." I'd made several additional copies. Not that the sheriff needed to know that.

She waited until I'd almost reached the door before speaking again. "Ms. Travis?"

I turned and looked back.

"Enjoy your Valentine's Day celebration in Steepleton," she said. "Eat chocolates, drink champagne. Have a lovely meal with your husband. And kindly leave the investigating to those of us who know what we're doing."

Chapter
Fifteen

Sam was talking about booking a sleigh ride on the way back to the inn. I was all in favor. But as we entered the lobby, Evelyn stepped out of her office.

She looked at Sam and said, "Do you mind if I borrow your wife for a few minutes?"

He glanced my way. Sam knew better than to speak for me, just as I wouldn't have spoken for him. I nodded and handed him Faith's leash.

"I'll be along soon," I said.

Sam and Faith hadn't even reached the staircase before Evelyn ushered me into her office. She shut the door behind us. Today, a fire was burning in the small hearth. The room felt close and stuffy.

"You were supposed to be keeping me apprised of what you'd learned," she said without preamble.

Evelyn's tone was anxious and there were dark shadows beneath her eyes. She probably hadn't slept well last night. Belinda's death was weighing on her. She had to be concerned for the welfare of her inn.

"It's barely been twenty-four hours since we spoke," I pointed out.

"Yet you found the time to go into town and talk to Sheriff Finley." She walked around behind her desk and sat down. "You must have learned something. Something that you should have reported to me."

That wasn't exactly the way I remembered our previous conversation. And how did she know I'd been to see the sheriff? Evelyn's assertive approach was beginning to grate on my nerves. Still, there was one piece of information I could pass along. She would know soon enough anyway.

"Belinda didn't die of exposure," I said. "She overdosed on oxycodone."

Evelyn's eyes widened. She lifted a hand and pressed it to the base of her throat. The blood drained from her face. "Are you sure about that?"

I nodded. "Sheriff Finley had just received the report."

"Belinda was an addict?" Her voice quavered. "I would never have guessed. Obviously I wouldn't have hired her if I'd even suspected she had a drug problem. This is shocking news."

"I agree."

"I know these things happen. But I never expected

opioid abuse to impact me personally." Then Evelyn sat up and stiffened her shoulders. "At least now we know her death was an accident, and that it had nothing to do with the inn. I suppose that's a small amount of comfort that can be derived from this terrible situation."

I remained silent as Evelyn continued to process the news.

After a few seconds, she glanced up. "Did the sheriff tell you where Belinda had gotten the drugs from?"

"I doubt that she knows. She seemed surprised by the results of the postmortem too."

Her question reminded me of something. The missing items that should have been in Belinda's room—items that might provide the answers we sought. If the overdose had truly been an unforeseen accident, however, how and when had Belinda's phone, purse, and laptop disappeared?

That thought was quickly followed by another. Not only were her things still missing, but there were a limited number of people who had access to Belinda's locked room—and I was standing across from one of them.

"What else?" Evelyn asked.

I'd intended to show Evelyn my copy of Belinda's list to see what she made of it. But now, suddenly, I wasn't sure how much more I wanted to tell her. Not until I'd had some time to think about the suspicions that were beginning to form in my mind.

"I know that can't be all you've learned," Evelyn prodded.

I cast around for another tidbit of information that might placate her. "There was one other thing. I heard that Belinda had been paying an unusual amount of attention to some of the recent guests. Do you think that could be something important?"

"I don't know," Evelyn considered. "Did you tell Sheriff Finley about that?"

"No, of course not." For the time being I wanted to remain firmly on Evelyn's side. "That was inn business. Nothing for the sheriff to be concerned about."

"Quite right," she agreed.

I knew that Sam and Faith were waiting for me up in our room. But now, when things were finally starting to make sense, there was somewhere else I had to be. I needed to talk to Belinda's best friend.

I sped down the stairs to the lower level. The bingo session must have already ended. Once again, the activities room was being rearranged. It looked as though there might be another movie later.

I walked around the corner to Jill's office. She'd left her door open, maybe hoping to draw some warm air from the hallway into the room. Jill was seated at her desk, a laptop open in front of her. She looked up as I paused in the doorway.

"Do you have a minute?" I asked.

"Sure. Come on in. Close the door at your own risk."

Since I hadn't been back to my room yet, I still had on the jacket I'd worn for my visit to Steepleton. "Can you deal with the cold for a few minutes? I'd rather speak in private."

Jill nodded. She closed her computer as I shut the door. "You have me intrigued. I assume this is about Belinda?"

"I have some further information about her death."

"Okay." Jill closed her eyes as if she was steeling herself to deal with it.

"Belinda died of a drug overdose."

"Drug?" Her eyes snapped open. "What kind of drug?"

"Oxycodone."

"That's not possible."

"I'm sorry to be the bearer of bad news," I said. "It was found in the postmortem. Evelyn said she had no idea Belinda was an addict."

"Evelyn's wrong," Jill replied firmly. "Bel wasn't an addict. I'd have known."

I sat down in the chair opposite her. "As I'm sure

you're aware, people who are dependent on drugs can be pretty crafty about hiding their habit."

"Not Belinda." Jill frowned. "She wouldn't have anything to do with drugs, especially not that one."

"What makes you so sure?"

"Belinda and I were friends. We lived practically on top of each other. We'd talked about our families. Bel dated a boy who played football when she was in high school. They were serious about each other." She huffed out a small laugh. "Well, as serious as things ever get in high school. He was her first. You know?"

I nodded.

"Senior year, he got injured and needed surgery. His recovery didn't go well—he was in too big a hurry to get back on the football field. Bel said he was in a lot of pain."

I could guess what happened next. "His doctor gave him oxycodone."

"He did," Jill said. "Back then it was the go-to prescription in cases like that. No one was worrying nearly as much as they should have been about getting addicted."

I sighed. "Is that what happened to him?"

"It was worse than that. The guy who was Bel's first love got addicted, then he got sober. Then he got addicted again—and committed suicide."

"Damn." I exhaled.

"Bel would never have touched drugs after that. I'm absolutely certain of it. If she overdosed on oxy, someone else must have given it to her."

Since I was on the inn's lower level, the spa was right around the corner. My copy of Belinda's list felt like it was burning a hole in my pocket. I still didn't know why the dates she'd written down were significant. The letters that followed them were equally baffling.

But after I'd left Sheriff Finley's office, something had occurred to me. Two of the letters—*C* and *H*—appeared twice on the list. When I'd spoken with Catelyn she'd told me that Belinda liked older guys. She'd pointed me in the direction of Cliff and Harley. *C* and *H*.

Maybe that was just a coincidence. But right now, it was the closest thing I had to a workable theory. Which meant that I needed to know who *J* was.

I stopped in at the spa and asked if Catelyn was available.

A chirpy receptionist consulted her daily roster. "Catelyn's out on her break. She's due back in ten minutes, but she's already scheduled for a massage. I can fit you in with someone else though. All of our technicians are great."

"Maybe you could tell me where to find Catelyn? I just want to have a quick word with her."

"I'm really not supposed to . . ."

My wallet was in my jacket pocket. I pulled out a ten-dollar bill and slid it across the counter.

The receptionist eyed the money. Scruples warred with avarice. It was a brief skirmish. The bill disappeared into the pocket of her smock.

"There's a door at the end of the hallway that leads outside," she said. "Catelyn likes to go out and vape every now and then. You might find her there."

When I opened the door, Catelyn was already heading back inside. A three-quarter length peacoat was buttoned up over her smock, and she had a yellow and blue striped scarf around her neck. She stopped and smiled when she saw me. "Ms. Travis, right?"

"Melanie, please. That was a great massage you gave me."

Her smiled widened. "I'm glad you enjoyed it. I'd be happy to schedule you for another if you like."

"Actually I have something else in mind." Gently I steered her away from the doorway. There were plenty of people outdoors behind the inn, but none of them were close enough to overhear our conversation. "Do you mind if I ask you something?"

"Umm, okay." Catelyn stuffed her hands in the

pockets of her coat. "But I'm due back inside in a few minutes and I don't want to be late."

"I'll be quick. Do you remember telling me that Belinda was interested in two guys here at the inn, Cliff and Harley?"

She issued a cautious nod.

"Did she ever mention someone to you whose name begins with *J*?"

Catelyn screwed up her face as she considered. "I don't think so."

"Is there anyone who works here whose name begins with *J*?"

This was apparently an easier question. It didn't require nearly so much thought.

"There used to be a guy," Catelyn said. "Jason North. He worked on the grounds crew with Harley. I can't imagine why Belinda would have been interested in him, though. He was a bit of a creep. None of the women who work here were sorry when he left."

"Where did he go?" I asked.

Catelyn shrugged. It didn't matter to her. "One day he was hanging around and the next he'd disappeared. Good riddance."

"One more thing," I said quickly. Catelyn was already turning to go. "You told me that Belinda had her eye on Cliff, but he didn't return her interest. Why did you think he wasn't interested?"

She looked at me as though I'd asked a dumb question. "Because it's true. Cliff is sleeping with the boss. There was no way he'd have given her up for mousey little Belinda."

"The boss." I gulped. "You mean Evelyn?"

Catelyn nodded, and then she was gone.

Dinner that night was a sumptuous affair. Though Valentine's Day wasn't until Sunday, guests at the inn—many of whom would be heading home the following afternoon—were celebrating a day early. We feasted on poached oysters, filet mignon, and mini red velvet cakes shaped like hearts. Champagne flowed like water. After dinner, there would be a sweethearts dance in the ballroom, which had been cleared for the occasion.

"You were preoccupied during dinner," Sam mentioned.

He and I had just come back from walking Faith. Now we were supposed to be getting ready to go downstairs for the dance. Instead, Sam and I were relaxing on the love seat in our room. I'd already had a busy day. The prospect of an equally lively night didn't seem that appealing.

"I just have a lot on my mind," I said. "I've spent the day trying to figure everything out and I'm not sure I have it right. But if I do, I don't know what my next step should be. So it feels like my brain is going around in circles."

"It sounds as though a bustling ballroom is the last place you need to be right now."

"Do you mind?" I looked up at him.

"Skipping a dance?" Sam chuckled. "Not in the slightest. I think I have a better idea."

I didn't know what he had in mind, but I was all in favor of Sam's good ideas. He'd never steered me wrong yet.

"Let's do it," I said.

Next thing I knew we were heading outside. In the dark. And the snow. Faith was tucked away safely in our room, and Sam was holding my hand. He must have planned ahead because he had two pairs of ice skates slung over his shoulder.

This would be interesting. The last time I'd been on skates, my age had been in single digits.

"I thought you said you didn't know how to ice-skate," I said.

"I didn't say I couldn't skate, only that I didn't want to join that wild melee after lunch." Sam's fingers squeezed mine. His grasp was warm and reassuring. "I've been waiting all day to get you to myself and now I intend to make the most of it."

Back in the ballroom, the band would be tuning their instruments. Women in silk dresses and high heels would be strolling around the crowded room with their partners. They'd be sipping their drinks and waiting for the music to start.

Out here in the moonlight, Sam and I had the starry sky and the skating pond all to ourselves. This was so *so* much better.

It only took us a few minutes to exchange our boots for skates. My feet started to slide out from under me as soon as I stepped onto the ice, but Sam reached out and caught me handily.

"Trust me," he said. "Let's do this together."

The moon was hardly more than a sliver in the sky, but when Sam put his arm around me, I felt as though I was lit from within. Together, we glided a circle around the perimeter of the ice. With Sam there to guide me, keeping my balance was easy. The skating felt effortless.

"You don't just know how to do this"—I gazed up at him—"you're good at it. How did I not know that about you?"

"A man's entitled to a few secrets."

"Sure." I laughed. "But not useful ones. There are zillions of frozen ponds in Connecticut. We could have been skating like this for years."

Sam's head lowered. His lips brushed the top of my head. "Or we could just concentrate on tonight."

I managed to execute a quarter-turn on my skates that sent me straight into his arms. Sam gathered me in with ease. My cheeks were pink with the cold, but the rest of my body was heating up nicely.

"That sounds perfect to me," I said.

Chapter
Sixteen

The four of us were in the dining room the next morning finishing our breakfast when a man came striding over to our table. He was of average height and medium build, possibly as old as thirty. His brown hair was cut short. His features were even and unremarkable. I thought he looked vaguely familiar, but I didn't have the faintest idea where I would have seen him before.

The man's gaze slid over each of us in turn, then settled on me. He stepped around the table to stand beside my seat. "I apologize for interrupting. Are you Melanie Travis?"

"Yes." I'd paused my coffee cup on its way to my mouth. Then I set it back down in the saucer. "Can I help you?"

"I'm Sean Linder, Belinda Rush's friend."

He paused, giving me time to make the connection.

After a few seconds, I did. Trina and Catelyn had both mentioned Sean to me. He was Belinda's ex-boyfriend. And now I realized that he'd looked familiar because he was the man from the photograph in her room.

"We need to talk," he said. "Now, if possible. It's important."

Despite his ordinary appearance, Sean Linder had the demeanor of a man who was accustomed to being listened to. He took my acquiescence for granted. Before I replied he was already stepping back, giving me room to stand up.

"Wait a minute." Sam looked at me. "Do you know this guy?"

"I know who he is," I said. "We haven't met before."

His gaze went back to Sean. "What's this about?"

"Nothing we can discuss here." Sean indicated the crowded room. "Are you Ms. Travis's husband?"

"I am," Sam replied with more force than I would have thought necessary. "Sam Driver."

"Perhaps I can speak with both of you upstairs?"

Sam was about to reply, but I beat him to it. I pushed back my chair and stood. "I think that would be a good idea."

"You're sure?" Sam asked.

"Yes," I said. "Let's go."

Frank and Bertie had watched the exchange in silence. Neither looked pleased by this turn of events. Like Sam, they were wary of our unexpected visitor.

"Call me in fifteen minutes," Bertie said. "If I don't hear from you, I'm going to come and bang on your door. And I'm bringing the feds with me."

Sean looked amused by the threat. "Do you know any feds?"

"No." Bertie gave him a hard stare. "But I'm sure I could find some if I had to."

None of us said a word as we went up to the room together. That was kind of spooky. Suddenly it felt as though there might be unfriendly eyes and ears everywhere. I trained my gaze straight ahead and kept walking. Sam stuck to my side, a welcome reassurance that if I was heading into trouble, he would have my back.

What was Belinda's college boyfriend doing at the White Birch Inn and what did he want with me?

Faith heard the keycard slip into its slot. As soon as we opened the door, she came bounding out to greet us. The fact that I'd brought her a piece of bacon from breakfast on the two previous mornings added an extra bounce to her step.

When she raced through the doorway, Sean immediately fell back. Then he quickly recovered. Seeing that she was just a dog—albeit a large one—he looked somewhat embarrassed.

"Sorry," I said. "I should have warned you."

"No problem." He ruffled a hand through her top-knot as we entered the room. "I like dogs."

Faith had already decided she approved of him. She accompanied Sean across the room. That was a good sign.

Sam and I both took a seat at the foot of the bed. Faith hopped up to join us. Sean sat down on the love seat across from us. Rather than making himself comfortable, he perched on the edge of the cushion, leaning toward us with his elbows resting on his knees.

"What's this about?" asked Sam.

At the same time, I said, "How did you find me?"

Now that I'd had time to think, I suspected I knew why Sean was here. He wasn't just Belinda's ex-boyfriend. According to the conversation I'd had with Catelyn, Sean also had a job in law enforcement.

He answered my question first. "Molly Ivers gave me your name. She said you'd been asking questions about Belinda's death." He inclined his head slightly. "Lots of questions."

I nodded. I could hardly refute that.

"Why?"

I thought before answering. Why did I feel driven to do what I did? It was a fair question.

"Because when Evelyn said that Belinda had died of exposure, it didn't make sense to me. She wasn't far from the inn when she died—so why wasn't she able to make it back inside? Also, I had seen her out there that night."

"You did?" Sean asked with interest.

"Yes. I told Sheriff Finley about it. Belinda was near the skate shack with the inn's lifeguard, a man named—"

"Cliff Granger," Sean finished for me.

"At the time I thought they were embracing. Now I wonder if he had his arms around her for a different reason. Maybe Belinda was already incapacitated and Cliff was supporting her so she wouldn't fall."

I stopped and blew out a breath. "I should have been paying more attention. I can't help but think that if I had done something differently that night, Belinda might still be alive."

Sam reached over and took my hand. His fingers closed around mine in a gesture of support.

"It wasn't your fault," Sean told me. "Belinda's death was caused by events that had already been set in motion long before you arrived at the inn for the weekend."

"How do you know that?" Sam asked.

"Belinda was an old friend of mine. She'd gotten herself involved in a situation here, and she asked for my help. Under the circumstances, I was happy to provide whatever assistance I could."

That all sounded good, I thought. *But Belinda had still ended up dead.*

"What went wrong?" I asked.

Sean sighed. "Bel could be impetuous. She leapt first and looked later. I told her we needed to slow things down. I wanted to be absolutely sure that we found the best way to approach the problem. But before I could make that happen, I got the news that she'd died."

"You'd known Belinda since college?"

"Yes, although we drifted apart after that. She and I still had friends in common, however, so we weren't entirely out of touch."

"Molly and Trina," I said.

"Yes," Sean replied. "Among others."

"Why did Belinda invite them to come to the inn this weekend?"

Sean frowned. "I'm not sure. If I had to guess I'd say Bel was getting nervous about what she was mixed up in. Maybe she just needed the comfort of familiar faces. Until she landed here last summer, Belinda lived her life on the move. I doubt she made many friends after college. The three of us probably reminded her of a more stable time."

Sam hadn't met Molly and Trina. He was still thinking about something Sean had said earlier. "If you and Belinda were no longer close, why did she ask you for help?"

"Because she knew I'd be the right person for the job."

"How so?"

Sean leveled his gaze. "I work for the strategic intelligence program of the New York Drug Enforcement Agency."

Sam looked surprised. I felt relieved. Suddenly it felt as though a huge weight had been lifted from my shoulders. Now I didn't have to worry about what to do next. Sean could take over and handle everything.

Sam had more questions, however. "You still haven't explained what the situation was that Belinda needed help with."

I stepped in before Sean could answer. "Several inn employees are using this place as a distribution center for opioids," I said. "They're bringing the drugs in from an outside source. Then, under the cover of various hospitality events, quantities of pills are being disbursed to some of the inn's 'special' guests."

It was still just a guess on my part. But based on what I'd learned, I figured it was a good one. Sam turned and stared at me. I hadn't exactly gotten around to sharing that information with him yet. Sometimes my husband slept better at night when he didn't know everything I was up to.

"That's what Belinda suspected," Sean told us. "And based on the information she'd been relaying to me, there were compelling reasons to believe she was correct."

I walked over to my suitcase, got out my copy of Belinda's list, and handed it to Sean. "I found a paper with these numbers and letters written on it in Belinda's room. Sheriff Finley has the original. I believe the numbers refer to dates."

"They do," he confirmed. "Belinda had been keeping a log. Once she figured out what was going on, she started tracking when the shipments were arriving at the inn."

"Every ten days?" I was shocked.

"The demand for illicit opioids is huge," Sean told us. "According to other sources we now have in place, these men were turning over thousands of pills a month. The letters on the list refer to the different couriers. *C* is Cliff Granger. *H* is Harley Jones. *J* is Jason North."

"Jason and Harley both worked on the grounds crew. That probably made it easy for them to smuggle things onto the property," I said to Sam. Then I turned back to Sean. "There's something else you should know. I'm pretty sure the White Birch Inn is having financial problems."

"Belinda didn't mention anything about that."

"She may not have known. It appears that Belinda was more concerned with when the drugs were coming in and going out. She was paying attention to Cliff, Harley, and Jason. But I suspect those three answered to the inn's owner, Evelyn Barker. Or—at the very least—that she was aware of what they were doing and taking a cut of their business."

"Evelyn?" Sam looked stunned. "But she's the one who asked you to get involved and see what you could find out."

"I know it seems odd," I said. "But think about it. This place must be massively expensive to run. And among the things I found out are that Evelyn has been having difficulty filling the inn's rooms. Also that she didn't honor the agreements she'd made with this weekend's vendors. Instead she coerced them into paying higher rates after they'd arrived."

Sean looked thoughtful. "It wouldn't be the first time that what looked like a thriving business was merely a front to cover up a narcotics operation."

I sank back down on the end of the bed. All at once, I just felt tired. "Poor Belinda must have been in way over her head. I assume you're aware that she overdosed on oxycodone?"

"Yes," Sean replied grimly. "I'm also aware that the drug that killed her wouldn't have been self-administered. That's why I'm here. I have every intention of seeing this investigation through to the end so Belinda won't have died in vain. It's the very least that she deserves."

Sam and I both nodded. Then Sean turned to me.

"You came in after the fact—and from a totally different direction—yet you reached the same conclusions Belinda and I did. That indicates to me that you can think on your feet when the situation calls for it. I'm hoping you'll agree to help me finish the work that Belinda started."

"What do you need me to do?" I asked.

"Not so fast." Sam stood up and moved between us. "It's all well and good for you to do your job," he said to Sean. "But Belinda was a civilian—and you got her mixed up in something that got her killed."

"No." Sean's reply was calm but firm. "Belinda is the one who put herself in the middle of this. What I was trying to do was get her out safely. Obviously I failed. But I'm here now, on-site, and able to oversee every step we take. That means things will proceed very differently. You can trust me when I say that I won't allow anything to go wrong this time."

Sam wasn't convinced. He looked back at me. "Clearly having anything to do with these people is dangerous. I understand that you want to help. But we should hear what Sean's proposing before you make a commitment."

"That's fair," I said.

Sean nodded in agreement. "When Belinda first came to me, I hoped there'd be time for us to work our way up the supply chain before we moved in and started making arrests. But her murder shined a light on an operation that was supposed to remain in the dark. That necessitates a new plan."

Sam crossed his arms over his chest. "Go on."

"I'll need to coordinate with Sheriff Finley and her team, but I have every expectation that she'll agree with me. We need to act quickly—before the players realize how much trouble they're in and evidence begins to disappear."

"Where do I fit in?" I asked.

Sean's gaze found mine and held it. I was sure it wasn't an accident that he'd excluded Sam.

"There's something I need you to do," he said.

I could feel my heart beating in my chest. It was almost as if I knew what was coming next.

"You're going to execute a drug deal."

Chapter
Seventeen

After that, things began to move with what felt like warp speed. It turned out that Sean had already put much of his new plan into place. All he'd needed was a willing participant to set the chain of events into motion.

Namely, me.

"This is crazy," said Sam. "There's no need for you to put yourself at risk for someone you barely knew."

"This isn't just about what happened to Belinda," I said. "It's about trying to protect the *next* Belinda, or someone's child who gets sucked into a life of addiction because terrible people exist in the world and no one stands up to them. If Sean thinks I can help him shut down this drug ring, I want to try to do it."

Sam frowned, then finally nodded. He wasn't happy, but at least now he understood why this was so important to me.

"I can't tell you there's no risk involved in what I'm

proposing," Sean said quietly. "But I can assure you that between my resources and those of the sheriff's department, we'll do everything in our power to keep you safe."

"I appreciate that," I said.

Sean outlined what he wanted me to do, and I readily approved. Sam's consent was more grudgingly given, but even he had to acknowledge that Sean's plan sounded solid.

Sean was on the phone with Sheriff Finley when Bertie knocked on the door. Apparently the fifteen minutes of grace she'd allowed me were up. Now she and Frank wanted to know who Sean was and what was going on. Sam and I gave them an abbreviated explanation, ending with the news that I'd agreed to seek out Cliff Granger and make a purchase from the supply of oxycodone that had recently been delivered to him.

"I'm going with you," Bertie said immediately. Before I could protest she held up a hand to stop me. "First, there's safety in numbers. And second, considering the encounter you had with him the other day, Cliff doesn't like you. So you'd have a hard time convincing him to do business with you."

She had a point.

"On the other hand," Bertie continued, "he's been flirting with me ever since we arrived—"

"He has?" Frank demanded.

"Oh shut up, Frank," I said. "Your wife is gorgeous. Every man with eyes in his head flirts with her. Get over it."

"Cliff will do business with me," Bertie said with conviction.

"But—" Frank began.

Bertie shook her head firmly. "This is nonnegotiable. I trust Melanie. She'll keep me safe."

"We'll keep each other safe," I said.

I had expected the air in the glass-enclosed dome where the indoor pool was located to be humid and smell like chlorine like the pool at the local Y where Davey and Kevin had taken swimming lessons. Instead the air in the tall enclosure was both fresh and warm. Now, in late morning, the pool was empty except for an older woman in a flowered bathing cap who was breast-stroking leisurely laps. A row of benches lined one of the tiled walls. There were two changing rooms, one for women and one for men.

Cliff was on duty, sitting in an open-weave chair at the other end of the pool. He was wearing deck shoes, swim trunks, and a T-shirt that was tight enough to display his toned body. He'd been scrolling on his phone, but he looked up as the door closed behind us.

No surprise, Cliff's gaze immediately went to Bertie. As we skirted around the pool, the statuesque redhead was smiling at him. She was also strolling with an extra sway in her hips. Her demeanor was so out of character that I nearly laughed. But this was serious business, and if Bertie could get us out of here quickly and successfully by flashing her charms, I was all in favor.

"I'll do the talking," she said under her breath as we approached.

Cliff's eyes shifted to me briefly, then quickly returned to Bertie. I'd already been dismissed as irrelevant. Under the circumstances, that was just as well.

"Hello, pretty lady." Cliff's voice had a low, seductive purr. "It's about time you took me up on my offer to visit the pool." His gaze raked up and down her body. "I hope you have your bikini on under your clothes."

"Maybe you and I can take a swim later," Bertie cooed. "But at the moment, I'm looking for a favor. I was told you were the person who could help me with something."

Cliff stood up and came closer. "Whatever you need, babe. I'm your man."

He managed to utter that line with a straight face. I wouldn't have been surprised if he'd punctuated the line by thumping his chest with his fist.

"I was hoping you'd say that." Bertie smiled. "What I need is a little . . . delicate?"

Cliff nodded eagerly.

"Is there somewhere we could talk privately?"

"Let's step into my office." He was already holding out his arm to guide her that way. Then Cliff glanced at me. "You can wait here."

"That's not happening," I said. "Bertie and I are partners. Where she goes, I go."

Cliff wasn't pleased about that development, but he strode to a nearby door and opened it. Bertie and I followed him into the cramped room. As offices went, this one wasn't much. Cliff's desk was littered with papers and his wastebasket was full. The fluorescent light on the ceiling flickered when he turned it on. Cliff leaned back against his desk and folded his arms across his chest. He waited to hear what Bertie had to say.

She began with another winning smile. "Melanie and I came here because we heard this inn was a place where one could access a certain profitable commodity." Bertie paused, but Cliff didn't reply. She stared at him for several seconds, then offered another prompt. "Prescription drugs?"

Cliff went still. "Drugs," he repeated, his tone giving nothing away. "I'm afraid I don't know what you're talking about."

Bertie leaned closer. "Pain management?"

Cliff shook his head.

"Really?" She straightened and stepped back. "That's too bad. If you had what I needed, I was interested in making a purchase. One large enough to make it well worth your while."

Cliff studied her intently for a minute. Bertie and I waited in silence. "You're going to have to be more specific," he said finally.

Bertie lifted a haughty brow. "Oxy," she said. "Is that clear enough for you? I was told you were the man with connections, but maybe I heard wrong."

She started to turn away. Cliff reached out a hand and stopped her.

"You've been here for two days," he said. "Why did you wait until now to approach me?"

Bertie tossed her hair. "I should think that would be obvious. Melanie and I aren't looking for any trouble. So when that lady dropped dead, we figured it was prudent to take a step back and wait to see what happened next. But so far . . . nada." When she shrugged, Cliff watched her breasts rise and fall. "And today's our last day. So it's now or never."

"The person who sent you here," he said. "Does he have a name?"

"Of course he does." Bertie smirked. "But you won't hear from me. You're not the only one who can take precautions. In your line of work, you should be grateful I'm the kind of person who knows how to keep a secret."

Cliff still looked wary. He glanced my way. "Your friend has made me an interesting offer. But here's the problem. I don't trust you."

"I don't trust you either," I shot right back. "And considering what happened to Belinda, I don't think you're very bright. But needs must. I don't see why a little mutual antipathy should keep us from doing business."

"Her death had nothing to do with me," Cliff ground out.

"So you said. Now let me explain something to you. When I spoke to the sheriff, I had no idea who the guy I'd seen with Belinda was. *And I told her that.* If I'd known it was you, I would have kept my mouth shut."

Cliff didn't reply right away. Bertie had done her job perfectly, but maybe I hadn't been convincing enough. I suspected we were losing him. The only thing I could think to do now was to walk away.

"Whether you like me or not doesn't change the fact that we're here with money to spend and you're stonewalling us." I turned to Bertie. "Let's go. This is getting us nowhere, and we're running out of time. Maybe we should—"

"Wait!" said Cliff. Greed was winning out over caution. Considering the business he was in, I wasn't entirely surprised.

Bertie was already reaching for the doorknob. We both paused and turned around.

"Suppose I could get my hands on your certain commodity," he said. "How much are you looking to buy?"

Bertie named the number Sean had given us. According to him, the amount was large enough to be tempting, but small enough to be doable on short notice.

"We have cash," Bertie said.

"You'd better," Cliff growled. "Meet me at the skate shack tonight, six p.m. Don't be late. I won't wait."

"We'll be there," I told him.

"Do we get to wear a wire?" Bertie sounded almost eager.

The six of us—Sam, Frank, Bertie, and I, plus Sean and Faith, were gathered in our room. It was five forty-five and already dark outside. I couldn't see the skating shack from our window, which was probably a good thing. Otherwise I'd have probably spent the afternoon staring at it.

"No wires," Sean said. "This isn't television."

"Then how will you know what's going on inside the shack?" I asked.

"Sheriff Finley borrowed an officer from the next town and dressed him up like a tourist. Earlier this afternoon, he slipped into the shack and planted a bug and several small cameras. Don't worry, we'll see and hear everything that's happening."

Sam, Frank, Bertie, and I had spent the intervening hours since the meeting with Cliff engaging in normal activities around the inn: eating, shopping, and even taking part in an afternoon Scrabble tournament. The afternoon had felt endless.

Sean had left the inn that morning shortly after Bertie and I got back to the room. He'd returned only recently, bringing with him a backpack filled with money and reassurances that all was going to be well.

"You won't be in any danger," he said for the second, or perhaps the third time. "All you have to do is exchange the cash for Cliff's drugs. As soon as that's done, we'll move in and take over. It's as simple as that."

"As long as everything goes according to plan," Frank said. "And there's no guarantee of that."

"Melanie and I will be fine," Bertie told him. "She has all kinds of experience cornering crooks. I'll just follow her lead."

Sean glanced over at me, surprised. I was sitting on the love seat with Faith draped across my lap. Sam was seated on my other side. With the two of them bracketing me, I felt secure. Hopefully I'd still be able to hug that feeling to me when Bertie and I left the room.

"Frank exaggerates," I said.

"Not by much," he snorted.

Sean stood up. He waited until he had everyone's attention before addressing Bertie and me. "Listen to me carefully because this is important. I need you to do exactly as you've been told. Don't make things any more complicated than they already are. Your husbands are right to be concerned. These men are dangerous. The last person who got close to their operation lost her life. Remember that."

Bertie and I both nodded.

"There will be people who have eyes on you from the moment you step out of the inn. Don't look for them. Don't look around at all. Just pay attention to the job at hand. I expect the two of you to be in and out of the skate shack in five minutes. Ten tops. Try to relax. Remember to breathe. And don't—either one of you—try to be a hero."

Sean's phone buzzed. He read a text, then motioned us to our feet.

It was go-time.

Chapter
Eighteen

The lights were on outside behind the inn, their reflection glittering on the snow. Even so, it looked dark to me. The weekend was almost over; most of the holiday guests had already left. Those remaining would be inside now, resting from the day's activities or getting ready for cocktail hour. The area around the skating shack was deserted.

Our boots crunched in the snow as we made our way down the path. I remembered what Sean had said about eyes watching us. The thought should have been reassuring, but somehow it wasn't. Instead my skin crawled.

Beside me, Bertie was strolling along as if she didn't have a care in the world. The backpack was slung over her shoulder. She was whistling a song under her breath. I didn't recognize the tune.

As if she'd read my mind, she looked over at me and said, " 'Camptown Races.' "

"You're kidding." I almost laughed. Maybe that was her objective. "Doo-dah? Doo-dah?"

"It sounds stupid when you say it like that," Bertie replied. "You're supposed to sing it."

"That is *so* not happening."

When I turned my gaze forward again, I saw that we'd walked farther than I'd thought. The rear wall of the shack was right in front of us. Its door was around the other side, facing the pond. I looked at my watch.

"Five fifty-five," I said. "I guess we should go inside and wait. I hope Cliff didn't play us for a couple of fools."

"I'm hoping the same thing about you," a voice came to us suddenly out of the dark.

I jumped, then spun around. Cliff materialized out of the shadows. He was dressed all in black, with a knit cap pulled low over his head. He was carrying a satchel in his hands. His gaze went immediately to the backpack. I imagined him licking his lips in anticipation.

"Let's get this over with," I said. Surely those unseen watchers would be as reliable as witnesses as the cameras inside the shack. "We can make the switch right here."

"No." Bertie's refusal was firm. "Not until I've looked inside the bag and seen what he's brought us."

"Same goes for me," Cliff said. "And out here, anyone could see us."

One could only hope, I thought.

We walked around the corner of the small building. Cliff pushed the door open and motioned for us to precede him inside. Plain wooden benches lined the windowless shack's slatted sides. A covered lightbulb hanging from the ceiling provided only minimal illumination. Dozens of pairs of ice skates, their laces knotted together, hung from hooks along the walls.

Cliff walked in behind us, but didn't close the door. A moment later, I saw why. Harley Jones came striding through the narrow doorway after him. Then the door was shut.

Bertie and I looked at each other. We'd barely gotten started and already things weren't going according to plan.

"This isn't what we agreed to," I said.

Harley squinted at me in the half-light, then frowned. "You didn't tell me she was going to be here," he said to Cliff.

Cliff was surprised. "You two know each other?"

"We've met," he grunted. "She was on the hayride, night before last. Asking questions about Belinda."

"What kinds of questions?"

"The nosy kind," Harley replied. "I don't like how this feels."

In the close confines of the shack, Bertie and I were forced to stand way too close to the two men. When Harley suddenly reached out, he was able to snatch the backpack off Bertie's shoulder before she'd even realized what he was doing.

"Hey!" She tried to grab it back.

Harley held the bag off to one side, out of reach. He unzipped the top and looked inside, then smiled.

"Did they bring the money?" Cliff asked.

Harley nodded.

"Did you bring the drugs?" Bertie demanded. "Because I'm not handing over the money until I see what you've brought."

"That's funny," Harley said with a snide grin. "Because it looks to me like we already have both."

Bertie and I hadn't even been in the skate shack for two minutes before losing control of the situation. I hoped Sean and the sheriff were seeing and hearing what they needed.

"Let's just make the deal and get out of here," said Cliff.

Bertie held out her hand. He started to give her the bag, but before he could hand it over, Harley pulled him back.

"Not so fast," he said. "How do we know these two are on the up-and-up?"

"Because we did our part," Bertie retorted. "Go

ahead and count the money. It's all there. Then give us the oxycodone and get lost."

Harley shook his head. "Something about this deal is giving me the heebie-jeebies."

Cliff turned and stared at him. "What are you talking about?"

"I'm talking about that one being mixed up somehow with Belinda." Harley nodded toward me. "It doesn't feel right. I think we should just take the money and go."

"You're going to *rob* us?" Bertie sputtered in outrage.

Harley laughed. It wasn't a pleasant sound. "It's not like you can stop us."

"What do we do about them?" Cliff asked. My stomach dropped. So far he'd had a moderating effect on Harley. Now it sounded as though he was coming around to Harley's way of thinking.

"Let's tie them up and leave them here. Those skate laces should do the trick. By the time anyone finds them, we'll be long gone." Harley reached for the nearest pair of skates and pulled it down from the wall. I began to shiver as he deftly began to unknot the laces. "Or maybe after we're far enough away, I'll call Evelyn. She can get rid of them the same way she got rid of Belinda."

Bertie's hand reached over and grasped mine. I was

pretty sure she was shaking too. I squeezed her fingers and hoped we'd been right to put our trust in Sean.

"You don't want to do this," Bertie said to Cliff. "Don't let him convince you to do something you'll regret for the rest of your life."

"Shut up, both of you," Harley snapped. "You girls aren't nearly as clever as you think, coming out here all by yourselves. Don't worry, you'll be a little cold at first, but after that Evelyn will fix you right up. All things considered, it isn't a bad way to go."

It felt as though I'd run through the entire gamut of emotions in the past several minutes. By turns, I'd been nervous, then frustrated, and then afraid. But now I was angry.

"Is that the last thing you said to Belinda?" I demanded.

Harley glared at me, his eyes glittering with malice. He pulled the first two long laces free and handed them to Cliff. "Belinda was already dead by the time I brought her out here."

"You dumped her in the snow like she was nothing."

"That bitch *was* nothing," Harley replied. "Just another stupid little girl who was too nosy for her own good."

His hand came up and shoved my shoulder. I stumbled back against a bench and lost my balance. My shoulder bounced off the wall.

"Put your hands behind your back so he can tie them," Harley ordered. "And if you don't stop talking, I'll find something to gag you with too."

Suddenly there was a loud crash. The slatted door splintered and flew inward. "Police!" Sheriff Finley shouted. "Stop what you're doing and put your hands in the air."

My knees went weak as a wave of relief swept through me. I looked over at Bertie and knew she felt the same way. We were probably thinking the same thing too.

Finally! What had taken them so long?

Later Sean explained that they would have broken up the meeting sooner except the more Harley and Cliff talked, the more trouble they got themselves into. Having them also incriminate Evelyn, and accuse her of administering the overdose that had killed Belinda, was an unforeseen but welcome bonus to the case the DEA would be building.

By the time I heard all that, I was back in my room at the inn with Sam and Faith. Both of them had welcomed me as if I'd been gone for days rather than a mere half hour. It had felt much longer to me too.

In my absence, Sam had packed our bags. Next door, Frank had done the same with their things. Rather than celebrating Valentine's Day with a romantic evening, the five of us would be spending it on the road heading home. That felt like the best idea I'd heard in a long time.

"There's just one thing I don't understand," I said when we spoke to Sean before we left.

By that time, Sheriff Finley had already taken Harley, Cliff, and Evelyn into custody. The trio had quickly turned on each other, spending much of the trip into town denouncing their partners in crime. Sean assured me that when the time came to press charges, both law enforcement agencies would have plenty of material to work with.

"What's that?" he asked.

"Evelyn was the one who asked me to look into Belinda's death. Under the circumstances, why did she do that?"

Sean grinned. "Apparently she didn't have much faith in your abilities. She thought what Bertie told her was a joke. However Evelyn *was* concerned about what Sheriff Finley might uncover. She decided it might be a good thing to have you running interference. She hoped that would distract the sheriff long enough for her to have time to cover her tracks."

"That's insulting," I said.

"Except that you proved her wrong," Sam pointed out. "Now Evelyn is the one left looking foolish."

Sean nodded. "Trust me, she'll have a long time in jail to think about that mistake."

*   *   *

We arrived home half an hour before midnight. Technically it was still Valentine's Day. Our house was dark. Aunt Peg, the boys, and our Poodle pack were already asleep. Bertie and Frank's minivan was parked at the back of our driveway. They quietly transferred their things from one vehicle to the other and left.

Sam and I remained in the SUV for a few minutes before going inside. Faith was asleep on the seat behind us, her nose nestled between her front paws. There was snow on the ground and frost on the car windows, but it was warm and cozy inside.

"I'm afraid today wasn't much of a Valentine's celebration," I said.

Sam smiled. "Actually the long weekend was great up until the last day. It was nice to have a chance to get away together."

"I agree." I leaned across the console and rested my head on his shoulder. Through the windshield I could see that the night sky was filled with stars. "I'd planned to buy you a bottle of wine. And maybe some buttercream fudge. Then suddenly everything got away from me."

"I can understand why single-handedly cornering a band of drug dealers might cause that to happen."

"It wasn't just me. Bertie helped."

chuckled. "I noticed. Frank spent the entire
you two were gone swearing under his breath
pacing around the room. They'll probably never
o on a vacation with us again."

I sat up and looked at him. "What did you do
while we were gone?"

"I cradled Faith in my arms and told myself I had
to trust that you knew what you were doing."

"That doesn't sound too bad."

Sam shook his head. "You're wrong. I wasn't any
happier about the situation than Frank was. To distract myself from worrying about what was happening, I finally decided to count up all the reasons why I
love you."

"Oh?" I asked with interest. "How many were
there?"

"At least a hundred."

"I don't think so. That sounds excessive."

"I know. I was as surprised as you are," Sam
replied.

"Go ahead," I told him. "Start with number one."

He pulled me into his arms for a long, lingering
kiss. "If it's all the same to you, I'd rather show you."